SEEKING PATIENCE

JOSIE RIVIERA

INTRODUCTION

To keep up on newly released ebooks, paperbacks, Large Print Paperbacks, audiobooks, as well as exclusive sales, sign up for Josie's Newsletter today.

As a thank you, I'll send you a Free PDF ... The Beauty Of ...

Josie's Newsletter

Did you know that according to a Yale University study, people who read books live longer?

READER REVIEWS

very difficult time rejoining the real world long enough to cook and shower! I read all day... and late into the night. I hated the fact the story ended. I want more more more! I enjoyed every character, the plot, the way it is set up and the way the entire story starts, continues and ends. This author is not one of my normal ones .... However, after this... I will look for this author! So buy the book and most of all, make sure you have time to read it without a lot of interruptions."

"I loved this story. The research and details were great. I. liked the ending. It was heartwarming. I cried a lot. I recommend everyone read this book."

This book is dedicated to all my wonderful readers who have supported me every inch of the way.
THANK YOU!

PRAISE AND AWARDS

USA TODAY bestselling author

CHAPTER ONE

*E*ngland, 1813

*L*uca Boldor had made a mistake—a *big* mistake.

"May God strike you all," he swore under his breath at the murderous band of rival Roma tribesmen gaining on him, ready to attack. He'd merely been looking for food for his tribe.

He pulled his ragged overcoat around his shoulders and made his getaway through the snow. Snowflakes fell thick and heavy, twice as fast as earlier that evening. Wind carried the drifts in wayward, wispy circles and thankfully concealed his tracks.

He could escape unseen. He'd become good at that.

Slipping on a patch of ice, he stumbled and hit the ground face first.

His voice broke in agony. He stifled a scream, because a man never screamed. Certainly not a Roma man.

Relying on sheer muscle to raise the lower half of his

body, he dug his elbows into the gritty, wet snow and crawled forward. Aye, a man didn't crawl, either.

But sometimes a man made exceptions to his own rules.

Advancing shadows split the stretches of dull white snow. Desperately, he searched his surroundings, knowing he was too easy to find. His body ached with the pain of a cruel beating. His breath, so cold a moment ago, burned in his chest.

Give up. But the thought was so inconceivable that Luca pushed it from his mind.

Instead, he envisioned the elders of his tribe foraging for food. They'd starve without his hunting skills and perish in a sennight. If he could only get them through another winter, he could improve their lot by moving them to the coast. Food was more plentiful by the sea and they wouldn't need to steal to survive.

Heavy footsteps crunched through the snow and Luca risked a swift glance over his shoulder. Marko, the leader of the rival tribe, and his men drew closer.

Blind panic rushed through Luca's limbs.

Past a swell of blackthorn trees, he spotted a ravine. He dropped to his knees and burrowed into the snow. Faster. Deeper. His nerves pinched in short, silent spasms.

Curse the frost for numbing his fingers. Curse his senses for deserting him. Curse the whole, damn, uncaring world.

He lowered himself into the hole and threw brittle tree branches on top. Then he peered through the branches and waited. The bleary figures of Marko and his tribesmen approached. A glimmer of moonlight lit the darkness and threatened to expose Luca's meager covering.

A persistent voice whispered in his mind. *Run. There's time. They won't see you.*

He grimaced. His restless body shifted. His battered leg stiffened, a reminder of his helplessness.

"Luca won't escape me." Marko's rough tone severed the

cold night air. "He claims he disappears like a spirit, but he's just a man."

A few men snickered uneasily and Luca recognized their voices. Killing was a sport for them. Despite the numbness, tiny hairs on Luca's nape stood on end.

Marko's booted toes stopped within a few feet of Luca's makeshift hole. The stench of his unwashed body filled Luca's nostrils and he held his breath until he thought his lungs would burst. His eyes watered from the cold, but he kept his gaze on Marko.

"Nadya is my woman and they've been meeting secretly for months. She was hiding our food and giving it to him." Marko didn't speak, he growled. Despite the cold, he wiped his sweaty face with dirty gloves, then kicked the blackthorn trees, rustling the brittle branches of Luca's covering. "No one betrays me. Nadya learned her lesson quick, and he will, too."

In silent rage, Luca squeezed his eyes shut to blot the unsettling images racing through his mind. If he'd known that Marko was going to beat Nadya, Luca would've stayed and tried to protect her. When Marko and his men had stormed into Nadya's tent, Luca had fought them, then gotten away. He knew his strength would be no match for a tribe of enraged, jealous Roma.

Luca tightened his fists, defying the impulse to shake off the burdensome branches and pummel the rival lord's head into the snow. He'd not allow Marko to escape punishment for senselessly abusing a woman.

Nay. Not now. He swallowed to quell the pain feeding his anger.

He was a half-breed—half-English, half-Romany. And when his strength returned, he'd seek justice the Romany way —swift and sure.

At thirty years old, he was a leader. A legend to fear.

"Nanosh," Marko shouted to one of his men, "We'll resume our search at sunrise. It's too dark to continue." Marko's footsteps receded. His men obeyed without complaint.

Luca waited an interminable minute before he pushed the branches off his snowy covering. He heaved his body out of the hole and sucked in a sharp groan at the needle-like pain piercing his leg. Then he crawled away from Marko and his men like a helpless, despicable cripple.

If he didn't find shelter soon, he might lose his leg. Then he'd no longer command the respect of his tribe. Then he'd sink deeper in his English father's eyes—if such a thing were possible. Then...Hell, then he might as well die, because there'd be nothing left if he were a broken and helpless cripple.

Every few feet, Luca stopped to catch his ragged breath and control the shivers wracking his limbs. He tried to flex his fingers but they had no feeling, stiff and frozen sticks that hardly moved. Wryly, he thought about the leather hawking gloves, an unexpected treasure he'd found on a dirt road months before. The English dandy who'd dropped the gloves in a busy London marketplace never missed a step, never bent to search for them. Just kept walking, probably to Bond Street where he could spend more coin, while his rich, ruby cloak billowed behind him.

Those precious, warm gloves. All smooth black leather and cream silk lining.

Luca had left the gloves back at his camp for an elderly tribesman to wear.

Wryly, Luca shook his head. He'd assured the tribesman he wouldn't need the gloves, but foresight had never been his forte. Throughout the night, he'd pondered the ironic joke the fates had played on him as he blew on his cold hands.

He crawled, then limped through the snow, grabbing a

tree branch to steady his gait. Beyond, a large, ungated home loomed. He focused on the flicker of oil lamps in the windows, the tall chimneys standing as sentinels on either side of the house.

He'd reached the outskirts of Ipswich.

He gripped the tree branch tighter, the icy bark biting into his fingers.

He should never have led his tribe here. This town always brought bad luck, much as it had brought bad luck to his Romany mother.

A weighty sigh brought an unanticipated heaviness to his chest. His mother would've loved being a proper hostess in a fine house such as this, serving tea with hot, buttered buns to her guests while she sat on a cushioned settee. Why hadn't he been able to give her these things?

The wintry wind swirled his cloak around him. He slumped against the tree, his torn boots sinking into the snow, soaking his feet. He wiped the wet snowflakes from his cheeks.

He still remembered his mother's fragrance, bergamot and roses, the precious oils she dabbed on her wrists each morning. Her soft voice still resonated in his chest, whispering of love, and beauty, and happier days. And then she'd died, abandoning him, and he'd struggled and sparred his way to adulthood.

"A plague on the English," he whispered, knowing the haughty aristocrats living in the grand home couldn't hear him. He loathed the idly rich and the privileged life they led, the desperation giving him no choice but to seek their favor.

"Luca."

His legs gave out. Dropping the tree branch, Luca fell to his knees and peered upward. The voice above him sounded youthful, deep, and familiar. He clawed through his hazy thoughts, trying to remember the child's name.

"I followed you out of Marko's camp. I know you were trying to get food for our tribe."

Luca kept his attention on the boy, his dearest friend since the boy was a child. "Pulko?"

He heard his own voice, slurring, sounding weak.

Tears streamed down the boy's face, despite a hasty swipe at his cheeks.

"Stop crying." Luca didn't have the strength to give the boy his usual friendly cuff because he needed to lift his arms, and his arms prevented his upper body from collapsing.

Pulko mopped the scraggly whiskers on his chin with his ragged blue cloak. "No one saw me. I'm fast and stayed hidden in the trees."

"Circle back to the tribe. Your mother will worry if you're missing."

"She's asleep." Pulko crouched beside Luca. "I'll stay with you."

Luca's palms flattened into the snow. "Your foolishness endangers the entire tribe. You'll give away my position."

"I won't abandon you," Pulko said. "I'll protect you."

"Protect the tribe. I don't need anyone."

Pulko hunched into his overcoat, his long dark hair flapping in the blustery weather. He paced, making a line of large footprints in the snow. "Marko will kill you if he finds you."

"Brush away your tracks and go. I'll seek help at the English mansion from one of the stable boys. Otherwise, Marko might capture us both and then our tribe would be lost." Luca grappled for the tree branch. With painstaking slowness, he braced his weight on his good leg and wobbled to his feet. He'd known Pulko all his life, two young males caring for an elderly tribe, bonded by shared responsibilities.

Refusing to meet Pulko's dark eyes, Luca drew his face taut against the wind and stared straight ahead. "Stay low and out of sight. I know what's best," Luca said.

He waited for the boy's brisk steps to wane, then forced a grim smile. Pulko knew better than to disobey. Luca was the tribal leader and his decisions, whether good or bad, safe or dangerous, weren't questioned.

When he was certain Pulko was gone, Luca leaned on his makeshift cane and wrenched his muscled body toward the estate. His temples thudded with the effort.

The woods thinned, exposing a field coated in ice.

Bone-chilling cold. Water soaked through his clothes and penetrated his skin. He sank to the ground. His dreamlike state numbed his wits and tempted him to curl into a locked ball.

His shoulders rose in a shrug of anger. Never. No man would ever find him in such a pathetic position.

Calm shrouded the air. He glanced at the sky. Soon it would be early morn.

The stable looked deserted and he pushed on. Bottomless purple clouds framed the imposing English home, the wood strangely weathered and neglected at closer range. A wide arch boasted an entryway. He doubted he could reach it.

~

Fight. But his body wouldn't stop shivering, his arms wouldn't stop shaking.

His heartbeat weakened, faded. Hopeless images of his tribe flashed across his mind, then images of happier times before the endless poverty and starvation.

Times such as Pulko and his sister running across a field, chasing a shiny, red ball they'd stolen from an innkeeper's barn. Pulko's sister had loved that ball, clutching it ever so tight. When the fever struck her small body she'd wanted the ball near, turning it round and round with her tiny fingers while she sweated and moaned in pain.

They'd buried her with that red ball, setting it beside her in the small wooden casket.

Joy was elusive and fleeting. If a person didn't appreciate it, joy slid through one's fingers as soon as one looked away.

Luca focused on his shallow breathing, one breath, another, another. The pain in his leg receded, becoming a dull throb on the fringe of nothing. He crawled the last few feet to the entryway of the large, English home and lost his struggle for consciousness.

CHAPTER TWO

*P*erched on a wingback chair near a cozy, crackling fire in her bedchamber, Lady Patience Blakwell sewed a row of uneven stitches along the ripped seam of her wool scarf. A simple task, requiring little thought and littler effort. She did a poor job, knew it, and didn't care, for no one inspected a wool scarf. But she tried to behave like the other ladies, at least a little, and every woman she knew sewed.

A wisp of stubborn hair loosened from the long, curly ringlets on her forehead and fell into her eyes. She blew the strand back with a huff. Her thick hair never cooperated with even the simplest style. She poised the needle in midair, tucked the offending strand beneath her mob cap, and peered out the window at the vast acres of her late husband's estate.

"Lord Bertram Blakwell, what a quandary you left me to sort," she said aloud.

The frustration rising in her throat spilled over, choking her.

If she remembered how to cry, she would have, although she hadn't cried since she was thirteen, and she had no intention of crying eight years later. So she did what she always did. She swallowed her feelings and buried them at the bottom of her heart where nothing could hurt her.

She glanced out the tall window, framed by sheer white curtains. A pink sunrise lit the blanketed, wintry fields. Perhaps the day would turn bright now that the snowstorm of the previous night had passed.

Patience accidentally pricked her thumb and put down her sewing, tormented by thoughts of her tyrannical late husband's endless speeches and lewd manner. When he was red-faced and yelling, she'd prayed fervently for strength.

At sixteen, her father had forced her to marry Lord Bertram Blakwell, the Earl of Orwell, assuring that the earl would give her prosperity, security and children.

Five years after the marriage she had neither prosperity, nor security.

Nor a husband. Nor a child.

With a weighty sigh, she set the wool scarf into the sewing basket beside her chair.

So much for neat stitches. She'd never liked sewing, anyway.

Voices from the hallway below halted her musings and she frowned. Unexpected visitors in the early morn didn't bode well.

She couldn't call for her lady's maid, Amelia, to assist her in dressing, as Amelia was visiting an uncle in Bucklesham. Struggling with the buttons, Patience quickly changed her muslin morning dress for a white satin slip and black mourning frock.

Oliver, her devoted lapdog, settled closer to the hooded fireplace and absorbed the scant warmth remaining in the bedchamber, the rest being carried away by the drafts. The old dog cocked his head, sniffed, and tucked his nose between oversized paws.

Patience stepped to him and affectionately scratched his ears. "Little help you'd be if I ever needed protection."

A rap sounded on her bedchamber door. Penham, the head butler and a trusted servant, stepped in and filled the room with his booming voice and portly body.

"Pardon, my lady. You're needed downstairs. There's a man in the hall."

"Another creditor?" she asked.

She was a dowager duchess, although the title meant nothing. The responsibility, however, weighed heavily on her. How was she supposed to maintain her estate on the miserly monies her stepson, Lord Crispin Blakwell, allowed?

Oh, if only she were done with this groveling. By dower law, she was entitled to one-third of her late husband's estate, but Crispin threatened to formally charge her with murdering his father and withheld the monies. She was forced to rely on Crispin's benevolence and live in her dower house, one of the lesser properties, until she proved her innocence.

And how likely was that? She was a woman, and a poor one.

"The man in the hall is a Gypsy, and Digby wants to send the Gypsy on his way. I told your steward that you're compassionate and gentle, and you've always cared for beggars."

Patience crinkled the pleats of the black gossamer dress hanging loosely over her hips. "If my stepson, Crispin, didn't force me to keep Digby on, I'd have discharged Digby a fortnight ago."

Penham nodded and gave a slight bow. "I wouldn't have disturbed you but—"

"You were right to come to me." She filled her lungs with a fortifying whiff of warm air. The aroma of fresh baked bread from the kitchen wafted through the bedchamber.

Her stomach growled and she shook her head. She couldn't control her hunger of late.

Walking to the bedroom fireplace, she carefully stepped over her sleeping dog. In two rapid breaths, she blew out a row of stubby beeswax candles on the cupboard.

Penham shifted. "This man downstairs, he's not well."

She tied her paisley cashmere shawl around her shoulders. "Show me to him."

He offered a slight smile. "Of course, my lady. You're a fine and brave woman."

She followed Penham's long, flapping waistcoat through the hallway and a hint of vinegary herbs assailed her nose, reminding her of her late husband and his unending medicine vials scattered throughout the house.

Patience reached the bottom of the oak stairwell, then jostled past several kitchen maids crowded in the hall.

A lifeless Gypsy man huddled near the entryway. He was rough looking, with strong, angular features, lying helpless in filthy clothes.

A cutting reminder of her late husband's battered body six weeks earlier returned in a rush and her breathing hastened. Perhaps the men who'd killed her husband were the same men who thrashed this Gypsy.

She rushed to the Gypsy's side, lowered to her knees, and lifted him by his forearms.

He groaned and crumpled against her, heavy, dirty, and pale beneath dark skin. Fearing she might drop him, Patience settled his head in her lap and lightly touched his wet hair.

Digby, her steward, regarded the raw-boned Gypsy with undisguised disdain. He sniffed and arranged the puffing of white linen at his wrists. "Rather appalling, my lady. A Gypsy beggar isn't the sort of person Lord Blakwell allowed on his estate. May I suggest that 'tis best if this man crawls back to where he belongs."

Patience halted the disdainful servant with a glacial glare.

"This Gypsy cannot walk, let alone crawl. I'll not allow this man, nor any man, to freeze to death outside my door."

She pressed her ear against the Gypsy's mouth, reassured by slow, faint breaths. His lower arms were bare where the ragged tan cloak fell away, exposing a well-muscled arm covered with black, silky hairs. Her gaze lingered on his large hands, masculine and scarred. So different from the shaking, gnarled hands of her late husband, or the smooth, pampered hands of her late father. Callused and rough, the Gypsy's hands were those of a rugged hunter.

A dangerous hunter.

Her fingers lurched. She had the fleeting urge to pick up her skirts and tear from the hall. But that was utter nonsense. With his brutal injuries, he could no more hunt than she could sew.

The Gypsy's eyelids snapped open, revealing a black gaze that stared straight through her. His nearness caused her overwrought nerves to crackle in awareness.

He jerked his gaze from hers, then swung back. Their eyes locked.

"Help me." His voice—an urgent twinge woven into a rich, low timbre.

She studied his set jaw and sharp profile. From the little she'd heard, Gypsies led perilous lives full of bluffs, brawls, and violence.

She hesitated, chastising herself for debating whether to aid him. He was badly injured and desperately poor, and she'd done all the cowardly things she could do in one life—bowing to the commands of cruel men who'd cared only about themselves.

She placed her warm hands on the Gypsy's cold ones, praying her decision didn't jeopardize her servants by placing them in danger. Most were house maids and possessed neither the skills nor experience to fight off an unexpected attack by ruthless Gypsies.

"With God's mercy, of course I'll help you," she said.

He closed his eyes. His long black lashes cast a straggled shadow on his cheeks.

Patience turned to her servants. "Penham and Digby, please lift the man to his feet."

Aching with sympathy, yet prudent enough not to let anyone see her concern, she stood and offered a reassuring smile to her recoiling housemaids.

"Allow us to pass," she said.

Patience straightened to her full height of five feet and pointed Penham and Digby toward the stairwell as she walked alongside. The Gypsy's lips whitened beneath his dark skin as he sagged against the sneering Digby.

No man would endure all this suffering in a guise to steal her insignificant assets. She almost opened her mouth to tell the Gypsy as much, but gave herself a hard rational shake. Life required choices. Hers was to walk with God and help the less fortunate.

Patience hurried ahead. "Bring this man upstairs to a spare chamber."

No footsteps followed and she wheeled around.

The Gypsy resisted the servants' attempts to move him. He groaned, a soft grasp for breath. "I'll not go upstairs. There's no time and I must leave. You cannot fight—"

Her gaze jerked to the Gypsy's face. "Fight? Fight who?"

Lines of pain etched into the corners of his mouth. "Tend to me here."

"Who is there to fear?" she asked.

"Tend to me here." The fierceness of the Gypsy's demand made her stop in mid-step.

"This is my house and I choose where to care for you.

Upstairs is safer because it will be harder for them to find you there."

"Nay. Cruel men search quickly—"

She stood ramrod straight. "The lawmen in the town will protect us."

He laughed, or snickered, she wasn't sure. "Fifty lawmen in fifty towns aren't enough."

"I have servants," she said.

The Gypsy shook his head. His straight black hair fell across his face. "Not enough."

He repeated the same warning twice, and both times the warning made little sense. This was a civilized England ruled by the Prince Regent, George, Prince of Wales.

"The citizens of Ipswich are law-abiding and honest, the town prosperous. The barristers and constables keep order and peace." Her shoulders went back. "I'm not afraid of anyone."

"You should be."

She narrowed her eyes at the sharpness of the Gypsy's tone. Several of her servants fell back amidst a murmur of disapprovals.

Digby's jaw was a hard, distinctive line. "My lady, may I suggest—"

"One more suggestion and I'll no longer require your services, no matter what my stepson says," she countered.

That quieted him. That quieted the entire room.

The Gypsy weaved twice as the servants hauled him up the stairwell and along the far end of the hallway. The oil lamps swayed and flickered as they passed.

Once in the chamber, Penham half-carried the Gypsy to the four poster bed.

Patience squinted into the dim light. Her late husband's vinegary medicines still lined the top of a mahogany wardrobe. Ultimately, he'd died from his beating, not his long illness. She tried inhaling through her mouth because the smell brought back memories she'd rather forget.

She shuddered and wrapped her thick shawl closer about her shoulders.

With flint and tinder, Penham lit a fire in the fireplace and two candles on the night table. Another servant bolted the tall, narrow window more securely to keep out the wintry morning air, and added a screen to lessen the draft.

A brown quilt lay folded on a stool beside the wardrobe.

Patience piled the quilt in her arms, brought it to the bed, and tucked it about the Gypsy.

"Who are you?" she whispered.

No answer. He was obviously penniless, although he had a noble look about him. She brushed her hands up his cloak, prompting convulsed shivers to rattle his body.

"You'll freeze to death if you stay in these stiff clothes," she said.

She turned. "Penham, begin removing this man's wet clothes. Digby, instruct the housemaid to fetch hot tea from the kitchen. The drink will warm the Gypsy."

Digby rooted himself in the doorway. He tilted his head, his gaze cold. "May I suggest, my lady, that you supervise Cook in the kitchen so that I, or one of the other male servants, may attend to this beggar properly."

"I'm assuming you didn't forget my earlier reprimand regarding your suggestions," she said sharply. Either Digby had a poor memory, or he didn't respect her authority.

She hung her shawl by the doorway, then twisted to face him. "I've treated countless injuries and have the skills to care for this man. Go and tell the housemaid to bring the tea."

"Perhaps—"

She raised her chin. "Perhaps you didn't hear me?"

Digby's thin lips folded in as he trudged from the bedchamber.

Patience pulled a stool by the bed. Lowering the overcoat off the Gypsy's shoulders, she gasped at the bruises along his neck. "Whatever happened to you?"

He didn't reply. His breathing was soft, interrupted by jagged gasps.

Carefully, she removed his tattered cravat and the green sash tied at his waist, then tugged off his worn boots and placed them on the floor. Penham raised the Gypsy's upper body and Patience lifted off a worn leather pouch strapped around the Gypsy's waist. His thin linen shirt and the orange scarf around his head followed. She winced at the fierce scar cut across the coarse hair on his chest, an old injury among his recent ones.

"How many brawls can one man be in?" she asked softly.

His eyes opened, but his gaze was dazed and unfocused. He moistened his lips. "Over a hundred."

Penham settled a pillow under the Gypsy's head, then folded the clothes and placed them on the wardrobe. "Lady Blakwell, I can finish here."

"I'll fetch clean cloths and hot water while you undress the man," she said. "Then I'll see to his injuries."

Penham's gape turned owlish. "Are you certain, my lady? Perhaps we should discreetly call for the physician?"

She met her elderly servant's gaze directly. "My uncle was a physician. I assisted him many times."

Patience hurried through the entry and closed the door. When she returned, Penham nodded toward the Gypsy on the bed, restless beneath a heavy quilt. With the subtlest of scowls, Penham withdrew from the chamber and latched the door behind him.

The logs in the fireplace sparked. The air was heavy with the scent of dried blood, as hard as iron. A hush filled the bedchamber and she shifted uneasily. Quiet moments needed to be filled with chores and chatter or unwelcome memories rushed to the surface.

She regarded his buckskin breeches, folded with his other clothes on the wardrobe, then turned to study his face. Just his face.

His full lips twisted cynically, even in sleep, although his rugged features softened as his breathing slowed. The fire warmed the room and drops of perspiration lined his forehead. He opened his eyes and attempted to speak, but his eyes closed as quickly as they'd opened and his expression shut down.

She touched his forehead. "You've endured much, but by God's divine power you'll be strong again."

Patience went to the hearth and gathered two pieces of linen. She dipped one in the warm water, the other she kept dry. Grateful that she stored her sewing notions in every corner of the house, she started for her needle and thread. She washed her hands, then the needle, then brought the needle to the fire in the fireplace to sterilize the tip.

By candlelight, she threaded the needle and went to the bed, then raised the bottom hem of the quilt to expose the Gypsy's torn leg.

She kept her gasp to herself while she eyed the gashes and washed him with clean linens. She blew on the cuts, then the needle. "Your wounds are deep and starting to fester." She bent her head and made a firm attempt to control her trembling. "Fortunately, I am...somewhat of a seamstress. You can trust me to stitch your wounds."

Her husband's sour herbs blended with the smells of the Gypsy's sweat and blood and unspeakable injuries. Her stomach roiled. Her hands shook as she lifted the needle.

"I'll do you no harm," she said, adding with an attempt to lighten her panic, "as long as I don't teeter to the floor in a swoon and miss the wound completely."

She choked gulp after sickened gulp as she forced her stitching through the tender, raw parts of his skin. She bound the dry linen cloth over his stitches and covered his lower body with the quilt. When she finished, she ran her hands over his muscled arms, his massive shoulders and bronzed chest. A tremor wracked his body.

"Father," he murmured.

"Do you call for our Father in heaven?" she asked.

The Gypsy shook his head. "*Gadje, Gadjensa, Rom, Romensa.*"

"I don't understand. Shall I fetch your father?"

"English with English. Rom with Rom." The Gypsy opened his eyes, his gaze so intense and full of hatred that it tore through her stomach like a broadsword.

She grabbed for the moistened cloth and swabbed his forehead and gashes as gently as her fingers allowed. His head tossed on the pillows. He rambled in his strange tongue, mysterious and indistinguishable Gypsy words.

"Ssh, try to sleep," she whispered.

"Marko." He grabbed the sleeve of her frock. His eyes darted, black, smoky fireballs that refused to rest. "I must leave."

"You cannot. Your leg—"

"Nay! Not my leg!" He screamed a hollow denial, ravaging her insides. He yanked back the quilt and tore at the bound linen cloths.

Her heart wrenched and she clutched his restless hands. "You won't lose your leg. I sutured the nastiest of the gashes. You just can't walk on it for a while. With time, you'll heal with few scars."

He stared down at his leg and his face hardened. "You've taken away my chance to escape."

"I saved you and you should be grateful." She released his hands, grabbed the quilt, and bundled his legs.

An ornate, ruby-red ring glimmered from his forefinger. Why did poverty-stricken Gypsies indulge in such colorful clothes and expensive jewelry? Perhaps it was a way for them to enjoy the small, beautiful things in life amidst all their hardships.

"I can't endanger you further," he said solemnly.

"You can't endanger anyone if you're just lying here. Don't fret. I'll protect us."

His mouth slipped to the slightest of smiles. "You don't look old enough to protect a puppy."

"My, you're such a flatterer."

His head fell back against the pillows and his hand found hers. He jerked her fingers to his face. "Is there something to quell the pain?"

There was laudanum, but she refused to use it. The medicine was too powerful and oftentimes deadly.

"Nothing will help for long." She spoke quietly, fighting for a balance of calmness and honesty, groping for believable reassurances. "The first few hours are the worst, but I'll not leave you. Give yourself time to heal."

"I have no...time." His voice faded, the suffering naked on his face.

Humming seemed to soothe him, so as the morning passed, all the English songs she'd learned as a child passed through her lips. Songs of fair maidens and faraway kingdoms —all dreams that belonged to other people's lives.

Over and over she ran the moistened cloth along the stubble of hair on his chin.

And she prayed. "Please, Lord, heal this man and take away his pain."

She squeezed the Gypsy's fingers, stroked his cheeks, wiped the sweat from his forehead.

He grasped her hands and held tightly.

The grayish morning pushed on in a blur. His moans

quieted. His breathing came easier. She stretched out her cramped legs and rested her cheek on the pillow beside him. Just for a few minutes, she told herself. Then she'd retire to a nearby chair.

His warm face dozed on the pillow next to hers. "Am I dying?"

"Nay." Lightly, she touched his chest. "God won't let you."

"Your God doesn't know me," he whispered.

She felt the Gypsy slipping back into his own, private limbo.

CHAPTER THREE

"*L*ady Blakwell, the only tea the housemaid found was green tea. I took the liberty of adding milk and sugar to the brew and decided to bring the tea up myself." Digby's voice came from the doorway of the bedchamber. "The scullery maids are a lazy lot, and the maid-of-all-work doesn't know a sliver of Pears soap from a slice of fresh fruit."

Patience blinked to rapid awareness. The Gypsy's heartbeat thudded beneath her fingertips in a slow, steady rhythm. His skin was cooler. She swiveled, taking in the brightness of the bedchamber. The time was well past noon.

Digby's disapproving face greeted her, and any remaining semblance of dignity she held was in shreds. Digby could easily report this to Crispin, and Crispin's opinion was crucial to her future. She jerked up and climbed off the bed so rapidly the stool overturned.

The servant flashed a cold smile, then raised a white porcelain teapot in one hand and two porcelain cups in the other.

Patience kept her back straight as she marched to the doorway. "Green tea is perfect, Digby. Thank you."

The steward lowered his chin. His gaze was shuttered. His mouth pinched. "Will there be anything else for your Gypsy? Hot water, more linen—"

Her Gypsy—comparable to her dog—like an animal she threw scraps to from her table.

"Nay." She accepted the teapot and cups from Digby's outstretched hands and set them on the tea table near the window. "Close the door as you depart and when next you enter, knock first."

The bedchamber door slammed, followed by Digby's footsteps stomping down the hall.

Patience turned to the bed and her gaze collided with a pair of perceptive black eyes.

She stiffened and clasped her hands together, polite and ladylike.

Absurd, considering the circumstances, a naked man on her late husband's bed, covered by little more than a brown quilt, his breeches draped on the wardrobe. If she accorded him the opportunity, she scarcely envisioned the tales he'd divulge. She only had to glance at his rough face to know he was a man of mystery and experiences better left unspoken.

"I didn't think you were awake," she offered.

~

"*A*ye, so it seems." Luca heard the weariness coloring his voice. He chased the weariness away with a ragged cough and choked groan. His mouth was dry, as if he'd been eating sand. He clutched the sides of the mattress until the quavering in his forearms subsided.

"How are you?" the woman asked. She looked so slight, so fragile, her huge blue eyes glistening with worry.

"Thirsty."

She smiled, an understanding beam lighting her heart-shaped face. "I have tea."

"Good," he managed, although ale would've been better.

He winced at the sunlight streaming through the window and squeezed his eyes shut, trying to shake off the cobwebs, thick and scratchy, blurring his brain.

She brought a porcelain teacup filled with tea to the bed and angled him to a sitting position. He felt her gaze on him as he drank greedily.

"Who's Marko?" She turned to the night table and refilled the cup. "Is he your father?"

Luca stiffened and opened his eyes. "Why do you ask?"

She placed the cup in his hands and steadied it. "While you were feverish you called out for Father. At first I thought you meant our Father in heaven, our God."

"You mean *your* God." Luca accepted the cup and shrugged off her hands. "And my earthly father is dead." Dead to me, he amended to himself.

"You dreamt of him," she said.

"'Twas a nightmare." Despite her questioning gaze, Luca refused to say more. It was the same nightmare that had tortured his sleep for years.

He'd walked with his father, at night, going on a fox hunt. One didn't walk on a fox hunt at night, one rode a fine horse during the day, but such was the nature of night-mares. He was three years old, but he'd assured his father he was old enough to catch the fastest fox in the forest because he'd made his own slingshot. They'd held hands, but his father let go and Luca was left alone. A fox lunged at him, its hot breath and sharp teeth nearing his face. Luca's heart raced, his hands shook as he'd tried to climb a tree. He'd screamed for his father, but the skeletal tree limbs far beyond his small hands ridiculed him by their distance.

"My father will search until he finds me," he'd assured the trees. "He'll not leave me to be mauled by a fox."

Luca always cried in his dream, despising himself afterward for his weakness. He could never shake the fear, the panic that gripped him afterwards, the emptiness of abandonment, nor the shame of defeat.

"Do you miss your father?" the woman asked.

Luca stared into his empty cup as though it might offer a plausible answer.

"'Twas simply a nightmare and it will fade," he said.

"I have nightmares sometimes." Those enormous blue eyes studied him.

He averted his gaze, handed her the teacup, and searched for a reply to appease her. He'd heard her voice while he'd slept, coming from a long way away. He'd doubted the voice was real, the tone so kind, so reassuring. No one had ever spoken to him like that. No one had ever reassured him that all would be well. Certainly never an Englishwoman.

"In your nightmares, do you fight off the evil villain?" he asked.

"Of course. The honorable are always victorious over the wicked."

There wasn't a hint of alarm or misgivings or disgust on her expression. Never in his life had an aristocratic lady looked at him thus. To the English, he was a dirty Gypsy, a person to loathe, a person beneath them. She could easily have let him die outside in the cold rather than rescuing him, but she'd courageously chose to save him.

If they'd met at another time, a time of less peril, he might have told her how much her kindness meant to an injured, weary man. If he could find those types of words.

She might have returned his compliment with a soft, self-deprecating laugh.

But he had naught to offer except his presence, which was

the last thing she needed because he placed her in grave danger.

Briefly, he closed his eyes, disgusted with himself for tarrying so long. "I must go. Help me stand." He attempted to swing his legs around the bed, wincing when a blast of pain split his side.

"I will not." Her spine straightened, and something changed in her expression. The gentle caregiver had vanished, and a stern opponent had appeared in her place.

He attempted charm. "I remember hearing you'd attend to my leg. Then you approached with a long needle and I passed out."

That brought a grin to her freckled face. "Hopefully not at the sight of me?"

"Nay. 'Twas your needle at fault."

"I sutured your leg as best I could. I'm not a physician, but I am a bit of a seamstress."

He ran a hand through his hair. "Are you trying to reassure me?"

"Aye." She leaned over the bed and smoothed the blankets. "Lay back so I may clean the gashes on your arms again."

"Promise you'll not hurt me." He smiled, just a little, but he wasn't jesting. He couldn't afford any further injuries if he wanted to leave quickly.

"You're hurt enough for one day," she said. "But by the grace of God, soon you'll heal."

He eased back onto the bed. Just for a moment, he allowed himself to believe her. Just for a moment. "Then I put myself in your care," he said.

She examined the wounds on his arms. Her expression sobered as she dipped the linens in the clear water. His blood stained the water. The levity passed.

"You slept a good while," she said, tending to him with the solicitousness of a mother cat hovering over her kitten.

His eyelids lowered, his arms felt heavy. "Shall I recite my dreams?"

"You're hardly able to keep your eyes open, much less speak about your dreams, although your speech is eloquent for a Gypsy."

"I studied at the finest schools, with the finest tutors."

"And I don't believe a word you're saying."

"The lovely vision tending to me is very real," he added.

"That part was a dream," she murmured. "Because, I assure you, I'm far from a lovely vision."

He gave in to the luxurious sensation of closing his eyes. "My strength often leaves me, but always returns."

"In the meantime, even the strongest men require rest."

He forced his eyes open. She was grinning at him, and he wasn't amused.

He lifted the quilt and examined his leg, neatly stitched and bound. How could he walk, much less run, without opening the sutures? He caught her anxious stare. Their eyes clashed.

"If there's one look I cannot abide, 'tis one of pity," he drawled.

"You mistake my expression. 'Tis one of disquiet, not pity. I've seen thrashings before, but yours was one of the cruelest."

He shrugged. "I can bear more than ordinary men."

Her blue-eyed gaze danced in the flicker of the candles. "And I can bear more than ordinary women. The secret is to think pleasant thoughts to fool the mind. I think of heaven."

"What is heaven?"

She hesitated, his question seeming to weigh on her. "Heaven is everything you love." Crisply, she smoothed the quilt over his leg.

Who was she, this aristocrat with the red scar across her cheek, wearing a black mourning frock? Her white English hands spoke of pampering, yet her eyes spoke of hardships. Whatever cruel accident had befallen her pretty face wouldn't prepare her for the kind of violence Marko would deliver if he found her with Luca.

"I must return to my tribe. Please. They need me," Luca said.

Please. He couldn't remember the last time he'd spoken the word aloud.

~

*P*atience fetched a linen cloth from the basin, but his urgency made her hesitate. She studied him, his dark handsomeness, his confident profile. And his manner, downplaying his injuries, gazing at her directly as he spoke, tilting his head as if to listen to her more intently.

He resembled a proud Gypsy lord, if there was such a man. He reminded her of nobility by the aristocratic jut of his jaw and the authority when he spoke.

Although that was mad. He was only a Gypsy.

Her fingers trailed the fringe of bed linens. This man, by his strong presence and good-looking features, made her self-conscious in her own home. Images of holding him, touching him, being touched, dreams dormant for so long that she'd forgotten such feelings, appeared. But she refused to let the images take hold. She shook them away, for they were as foreign to her as he.

His eyes captured hers. "Will you see to the gashes on my arms?" he asked.

That same stubborn strand of hair fell from her mob cap and half-covered her face. She pushed it back in place as unwelcome warmth started up her face and seared her ears.

The man was hurt and all she thought about was her own discomfiture.

"'Tis impossible for a mere human to heal someone in a few hours," she murmured.

"Make it possible," he said.

From the foot of the bed she retrieved a silk pillow and tucked the pillow beneath his head, wondering why she didn't stride from the room like a sensible woman and direct a male servant to finish the task of attending to the Gypsy.

She stole a cautious perusal at the medicine vials lining the wooden wardrobe. Two fortnights ago she'd done just that—counted on a servant, left the bedchamber, and consequently lost her husband.

Perhaps the Gypsy read her thoughts because he grabbed her hand to stop her movements. His hold was different than before, now more self-assured and bolder. No longer was he the feverish man squeezing with an intensity born of survival, in search of a lifeline.

His generous smile flicked a tremble down her spine. "*Kamadiyo*, I want you alone to tend to me."

She tipped her head nearer his mouth, expecting an explanation for the strange word. When one wasn't forthcoming, she said, "Sir, I wish to learn your name."

"Luca Boldor." His hand lingered. An overwhelming silence filled the air, as if he'd told her too much about himself, although he'd only said his name.

"Allow me to finish tending to your wounds, Mr. Boldor." The unfamiliar name drifted on her tongue, shadowy and unsafe.

"What is your name, *kamadiyo*?"

She permitted herself to peer into his fathomless eyes, although the warmth in his gaze threatened to dash any attempts at reason.

"Lady Patience Blakwell," she said. "I'm a widow."

"Lady Blakwell, the young widow." He smiled again, but this time it came slow and hinted of insolence. "I'm in the company of a true English lady. Shall I bow, or kiss your hand, or offer my sincere condolences?"

She reexamined the wounds on his arms. "You may stay quiet and do nothing."

Keenly responsive to his grimaces and sharp intakes of breath, she gentled her touch.

"How bad?" he asked.

"Your skin is dry and the wounds are clean."

"Shall I be grateful you're not the type of woman to swoon at the sight of a gash?"

"Swooning is for naive English damsels. I'm years past that nonsense."

"Lucky me."

"And unlucky me, for having the likes of you drop uncon-scious on my doorstep." She exerted light pressure on one particularly angry welt on his forearm. "Try to hold still."

His face grew drawn. He seemed to make a concerted effort not to flinch.

"The gouge on your leg is ghastly," she said. "Your stomach and chest are dreadfully bruised, although not cut." She spoke evenly to divert his attention from the pain. "'Tis too soon to determine if your leg is broken or badly sprained, since it looks to have taken the worst of the blows. Who did this to you?"

"No one you know."

The smoothness of his voice unnerved her. "A secret?" she asked.

He half-smiled. "I want you to be safe."

Heat vibrated from his body. Her hands fidgeted. He was all secrets and little information.

"Be calm, Lady Blakwell. I'm the one hunted, not you."

"And I have a hunted man in my home."

"And that is why you must hurry. My tribe will perish without me." Propped against the pillows, he seemed so confident, although they both knew he was very weak.

She shot him a dubious look and pulled up the stool. "You shan't travel far, so your tribe will have to wait."

"They can't wait long. They need me."

She frowned. He expected her ministrations to heal him quickly and her skepticism didn't seem to deter him. Before she could turn up the plain long sleeves of her frock, raging male shouts resounded from the hallway below, both harsh and unfamiliar.

Patience gave a momentary scan of the bedchamber door. "Who—"

Luca snared her wrists. "Marko and his vile men are here, searching for me."

She tried to yank her hands away and press them to her stomach, where her fortitude had quickly dissolved. "Marko is the man who thrashed you? Is he your secret?"

Luca held her hands firm. "Instruct them to depart before your servants reveal I'm here. I'll not perform a dance of death for my enemies, and neither will you. I was offered food for my tribe by someone trying to help me. I did nothing wrong."

His jaw tensed as he spoke and her mind sorted the facts beyond Luca's declaration of innocence. He was too injured, too anxious. He'd say anything, do anything, promise anything, to get back to his tribe.

"I'll not lie," she said. "Speak to these men as one reasonable man to another."

"Marko?" Luca's laugh was gruff. "He's a barbarian. He'll kill everyone in your home if he suspects you took me in. You must lie, for my sake as well as yours. Deter him, find an excuse for him to leave. I'll protect you if things turn bad."

Perhaps he could protect her if he could walk. Patience

looked around, grateful she hadn't said the words aloud. She glimpsed more than a twinge of unease in Luca's pleading expression.

Her gaze slid to the sunlight slipping through the bolted window while she contemplated her decision.

She stood. "I'm going downstairs," she announced.

"Please lie to Marko," he repeated.

Luca's demeanor had changed, now more serious, bearing little resemblance to the soft-spoken, teasing man of a few moments ago.

He expected her to do his bidding. On his terms. In her house.

She kept her voice steady. "I'm a very poor liar." She cinched the high waistline of her frock and straightened the demi-train. For the second time that day, she clicked a bedchamber door shut and quickened her steps to the hall.

CHAPTER FOUR

*P*atience reached the bottom of the stairs and held her breath. Two filthy Gypsy men stood silent. Their colorful cloaks were caked with dirt and stretched to span bulky arms and hulking bodies. Two pairs of bloodshot gazes impaled her across the length of the hallway.

She clutched the baluster and reared back. The wooden floorboards creaked as she scanned the drawing room. Digby, his posture stiff behind a straight-backed chair, flashed her a cold smile.

Beyond, in the dining room, honey cakes and tea were set out for a light midday meal, the scent of ground ginger and saffron unmistakable. Cook, Penham, and several servants stood near the kitchen doorway.

Digby stared at Patience with a hard squint, then adjusted his fancy waistcoat. "As you can see, we have visitors, my lady."

With a cursory nod, she acknowledged the larger of the two Gypsies, a frightening looking man with a long, stringy, black beard.

"I heard the disturbance from upstairs," she said to the

large Gypsy. Despite her efforts, the quake in her voice betrayed her nervousness. "What is your interest, sir?"

"We seek a Roma man, my lady. He's injured and we believe he's here." The man's polite words didn't match the derisiveness of his tone, nor his gruff, unwashed appearance.

She linked her hands in front of her. "You're mistaken." She swallowed her inquiry as to what had prompted his suspicions and stayed silent.

The bearded Gypsy advanced through the drawing room in four bold strides and stopped within a foot of her. He blotted his perspiring forehead with a wrinkled handkerchief and kept his stance wide. "No one lies to Marko."

Marko. The barbarian. The killer. Patience's blood ran like an ice-cold stream through her veins. She raised her shoulders, repositioning her body as a barrier blocking the stairwell.

"You're not aware of this man's whereabouts?" Marko shouted.

"Should I be?" she asked carefully. Her calves scraped the blunt ledge of the bottom stairs. She swayed but held firm.

He drew closer, forcing her to take in the uneven scar on his jaw, the odor of his rotting teeth. "His wounds led us right to your door. This man bedded my woman, then convinced her to give him food for his tribe."

Patience pasted her lips into a steely smile and mentally ran through the situation. Luca's battered body, his brave demeanor despite his injuries, his desperation. Maybe he'd bedded Marko's woman. Maybe he'd accepted food for his tribe that this woman had freely given. Or maybe Marko was believing that Luca had stolen the food, Marko's version of what had really happened.

In any case, Luca had obviously risked his life for his tribe. And Marko was obviously cruel in his beatings. In addition, Marko's manner towards her was threatening and abrasive, whereas Luca had been concerned about her safety, his manner polite and soft-spoken.

"The man you seek must be elsewhere," she said.

"Shall I summon the others, Marko?" the second Gypsy shouted from the hall.

"Don't call for your men, Marko. Leave at once." With a quick mouthful of air, she counted the cluster of servants huddled near the kitchen. Adding herself and Penham, they totaled six against two Gypsies, giving her and her servants the decided advantage.

Marko thumped his fist into his palm. "I command, little lady. Not you."

Patience tried not to flinch, although her heart beat so loud surely everyone in the house heard. She glanced around. No one moved.

She was much stronger than this, she chided herself.

"You issue no orders in my house." Her stomach knotted with fear although the outward breath she drew was brave. Her gaze sifted through the rooms, looking for one valiant servant willing to meet her eyes. In response to her silent appeal, Penham nodded and lurched forward.

In contrast, Digby's darting dark-gold eyes, like a frenzied fox, met hers. "Don't be foolish." He mouthed the words.

She glanced at the door. The other Gypsy man, face impassive, arms folded over his pot belly, barricaded the entrance.

Marko's glower narrowed on Patience. "Where is he?"

She stalled, refusing to draw back although Marko's chest was within a foot of her.

"Stay away from me," she challenged, throwing down the gauntlet. A portrait of Luca blazed through her mind. His feverish moans, his hand tightening around hers. He was a brave man caring for his tribe, not part of this group of repulsive men. Luca's manner carried authority, coupled with gallantry and courageousness.

Marko goggled the high neckline of Patience's mourning frock, stared at her face, and broke into a lecherous chortle. "This man hides wherever there is a woman—any woman will do, even a face on a stick."

She bridled at the insult but didn't rise to his sneers. She was far from beautiful. Her body was scrawny and a thin scar ran along her cheekbone.

Long ago, her adolescent declarations of love and clumsy attempts to please her smooth-talking cousin had brought only laughter and disdain from him afterwards. That, and his cruelty, for he'd burned her face with a tallow candle as a remembrance of their first and only night together. She'd endured the snickers and resulting scandal by building a tidy wall around her feelings, so high and so thick that no one could penetrate her heart.

"The man you seek isn't here," she scoffed, realizing a small dose of gratification when Marko's laugh faltered.

Marko's mammoth hand seized her shoulders. "I'm never wrong about my enemies."

She squirmed, refusing to cry out. "I told you to be on your way."

Penham charged forward. "Leave us as Lady Blakwell commanded."

A tide of servants surged. Flashes from Marko's silver dagger and splitting blows erupted.

One of the Gypsy men's heavy fists smashed into Penham's nose. Penham staggered and fell to the floor. He wiped the blood from his nose and looked up at Patience. With calm focus, he said determinedly, "Be brave, Lady Blakwell. 'Tis a small injury, and nothing that I can't tend to later."

Before she could respond, another servant plowed to the

fore, head down, fists drawn. Marko sent the servant reeling with an unpitying ram to the servant's jaw.

Patience heard herself scream. Time surged, slowed, surged again. She never should've let her foolhardy pride endanger her servants.

Marko brushed his palms together—a man ridding himself of numerous nuisances. She countered his blood-thirsty glare with her own dispassionate one.

"You have no business here," she said.

"This man is my business." Marko's tone, without emotion, chilled the hairs on her scalp. He peered over his shoulder. "Nanosh, open the door."

The entry door flung open and three Gypsy men converged into the house and up the stairwell, knocking Patience and her servants aside as they passed.

"Where is he?" Marko howled as she reached the top stair. Her gaze fixed on his booted feet, the cracking of door after door as he stormed down the wide-planked hallway.

"Stop! Leave us!" She launched at him and wrenched the seam of his cloak. "I'll notify the constable of this outrage."

"The constable owes me money. He'll look the other way."

One swipe of Marko's sizable knuckles snapped her head back. Her chin crashed against the wall in an explosion of white agony. She swallowed the bitter taste of blood and slid to the coolness of the floor. Her fingers crammed into tight-fisted pellets and she counted to ten through a swell of cramps shooting through her stomach.

She peered upward. A malicious grin crept across Marko's mouth.

Glaringly aware she had less than an instant, she curled her arms around her head and lifted her legs. She prayed she was strong enough for the unforgiving kick she planned to strike to his knees.

As quickly as her legs lifted, Marko caught her ankles. His

thick lips swam above her, his terrible voice belting his fury. "Show me to him or my men will bar all the doors in your miserable house and set every chamber ablaze."

"Please. Please wait." Patience tried to say more but she was shaking so badly her words locked in her throat.

Marko dropped her legs to the floor.

Slowly, she pushed to her feet. The stucco ceiling pulsed and weaved as she struggled for balance and she groped the wall to steady herself. Beyond, Luca's bedchamber door squeaked open, swinging back and forth.

Marko snatched a clump of her hair. Her pinned ringlets loosened and unraveled, sending auburn waves fluttering over her shoulders and her mob cap falling to the floor.

Marko dragged her past her private bedchamber. She prayed that Oliver's keen bark didn't sound from wherever he might be hiding. She swallowed, longing to glimpse the sight of her dog's pricked ears, knowing she couldn't reach him. He was so small, so loving, with huge trusting brown eyes. She couldn't protect him now. She couldn't protect anyone. Not her servants, not Luca, not herself.

Marko's bulbous shape and Patience's slight one cast a shadow on the floor as they entered the last bedchamber in the hallway. Luca's bedchamber.

For an entire morn, she'd tried to save him, a man she hardly knew. All for naught.

These men would show no compassion when they found Luca lying helpless on the bed. Everything had gone mad and he was at the center of the madness.

Gradually, her eyes adjusted to the watery sunrays lighting the bedchamber. An afternoon wind howled and cold air whistled through the unbolted window. One lone, discarded pillow lay bunched on the floor.

Incredulity stopped Patience from breathing. Open-mouthed, she dragged her gaze to the empty bed. Luca had vanished.

Marko released his grip. "Where is he?"

She heard his voice from a long way off. Strange. She never swooned, but her knees shook, her ears buzzed, her blood surged. She groped the top of the wardrobe, sweeping her late husband's medicine vials to the floor. She knew she was falling, heard the shattering of glass around her. Her thoughts swirled white, then black, shouting far-off denials.

Luca had quit the bedchamber.

Impossible.

CHAPTER FIVE

*P*atience forced her eyelids open, licked her cracked lips, and stared up at Marko.

He wrested her from the oak floor. She stumbled and landed against the wall.

He threw the draperies open and the window wide, then leaned over the ledge. "Indeed, 'tis a cold month to keep your window unbolted, little lady."

If Marko spotted Luca's body far below, he gave no sign. He stood motionless and grappled the windowsill. After an eternity, he whistled a frustrated curse through his teeth, slammed the window closed, and swerved round.

To hide her trembling, Patience stooped to brush pieces of broken vials to the side of the room. Could Luca have crept out the window in his condition? Gypsies were notorious for their spells and curses, but even Luca couldn't get dressed, leap out the window, and float into the forest on empty air. He could hardly move, let alone walk.

Or could he?

Her gaze flitted to the half-open doorway and her heart plummeted. Nanosh and the other three Gypsy men prevented her servants from entering the bedchamber. She looked for Penham, but he wasn't there. Nanosh gave an ugly laugh and lifted a pistol from his overcoat, an apparent toast to her entrapment.

She rose and faced Marko in a worthy imitation of indignation. Her pride didn't permit her to remain hunched over like a servant. "As you can see, no one's here," she said.

Somehow, she withstood the impulse to shove past Marko and scan the fields, hoping, praying, to glimpse Luca vanishing into the woods alongside a hobbling Oliver.

Marko bent and examined a telltale speck of blood on the floor. He lifted his head and assessed her, intent on a truth she prayed wasn't emblazoned on her forehead in screaming scarlet.

He stood. "Who was the knave in this bedchamber?" he demanded.

She pinned a cast of annoyance on her features. "No one."

With a quietness belying their size, the Gypsy men strode into the bedchamber and encircled her. So casual. So menacing. So dangerous.

She balled her icy hands at her sides and gulped back the fear inundating her.

"A scullery maid cut herself in the kitchen several fortnights ago and used this bedchamber to convalesce," she lied.

"A scullery maid sleeps on a pallet in the basement. I know your grand English ways."

"And I pricked my fingers while sewing in this bedchamber." She spread out her fingers, forever jabbed by needles. "I'd forgotten."

The Gypsy men hung back, no doubt waiting for her to throw herself at Marko's feet and scrawl a confession. Marko tried to scare her by bragging that he could control the lawmakers. But he still needed information about Luca's whereabouts, and she could play a game equally as perilous.

She cast Marko a look of seemly resignation. "I tire of your degrading insults and threats."

Marko shrugged, turned toward his men, and ordered them to block the doorway.

She picked up the silk pillow, along with a piece of slivered glass from the vial. The glass felt sharp, finely honed, and polished. Sharp enough to deter a brutal man and protect herself.

Clutching the vial beneath the pillow, she stood on legs she hoped wouldn't abandon her.

Marko turned from his men and sauntered nearer her. "I expect payment for stretching my men to exhaustion." His tone lowered, sending an awful sting of warning along her spine.

She kept her lips sealed and hugged the vial and pillow to her chest.

With lightning speed for such a large man, he grabbed her shoulders.

"You filthy monster," she spat, shaking him off and landing a sturdy, knee-jerk to his thigh. "Release me!"

"English witch!" he thundered, whether from astonishment or pain she wasn't sure.

She clinched her hands beneath the pillow and accidentally jabbed her forefinger on the broken vial. A drop of blood seeped through her fingers.

Marko's gaze veered toward the bed. He yanked off his cloak and hurled her onto the bed so violently, the pillow and vial flew from her hands and scattered across the floor.

He eyed the broken vial. "Trying to kill me?" He laughed and fumbled with the ties of her frock.

A sheer black quake ended her final bit of sanity. Bile heaved in her stomach. "I demand you leave," she cried.

"Shut up." He wrapped his hands around her neck, crushing and squeezing. Her eyes closed to blot out his vile breath and mottled features while her teeth chattered and her senses dulled. Pervasive, sickening odors invaded her nostrils. She tried to distance herself, tried to ignore the Gypsy men's snickers by the doorway, tried to hold onto reason. A quiet moan, a woman's gasp, but it couldn't be hers, for she couldn't breathe.

"Marko."

A gruff voice broke through her horror and revulsion. Marko twisted to the side and swore at the large Gypsy man barreling into the bedchamber.

"One of our men spotted footprints leading to the river," the man shouted.

Marko released her and plowed to his feet. "Luca!"

Patience didn't swallow, nor move, nor adjust the ties on her frock.

Marko whipped around, sneering at her while he pulled on his overcoat and knotted his purple sash. A black line of hate ran across his face.

"I'll search these grounds until I find him," Marko said.

She thought she reacted to his threat with a short nod, although she wasn't certain.

She heard Marko and his men drive her servants down the hallway, although she didn't lift her head. She quivered from shock and degradation like the shattered, adolescent girl she'd once been, helpless beneath her smooth-talking cousin.

She rubbed her tear-filled eyes. Then she climbed off the bed and found herself crouched on the floor, searching blindly for a useless, shattered vial.

CHAPTER SIX

*P*atience attempted to walk the short distance to the bedchamber door, although her body refused. Sharp tremors stilted her movements. With a groan, she sank onto the bed and huddled, her face in her hands. Perhaps she'd passed beyond fear and outrage. After all, unreality surrounded the entire day.

Footsteps rumbled downstairs. Several minutes later, the babbling of servants intermingled with Marko's fading shouts.

The front entry door slammed and all was silent. Wretched, wretched silent.

Shakily, she stood and shuffled to the doorway. She needed to reassure her panicked servants that she was unharmed. Instead, she secured the door, leaned against it, and allowed the door to prop her up. Her hands still trembled. Her lips were still dry. Her feet shambled back to the bed, scattering snow and dirt from the Gypsy men's boots in wayward directions, exposing sprinkles of blood. She floundered to her knees and inspected every drop. Slowly, ever so slowly, she followed the trail of blood to her unused sewing closet adjoining the bedchamber. She rocked to her feet, pushed aside the wooden chair hiding the latch, and wrenched open the closet door. Slivers of dust floated through the air.

Oliver looked up at her.

Patience gaped into the darkened area. How had her dog gotten into the closet?

She blinked once, twice, and tapped her shaky hands on her thighs. She'd thought her dog was dead, swallowed into the forest alongside a floating Luca. However, Oliver's body waggled, all ardent adoration. In four tiny leaps, the dog reached her. Alert, shiny eyes and a rough, wet tongue reassured her that Oliver was very much alive.

Reason fought to reappear. She stroked Oliver's satiny nose and sank her face into his brown fur. "I'm so relieved you're safe." Clutching the dog close, she twirled in a circle, then stopped to view the small closet. Spools of thread overflowed the open lid of a large wardrobe, crammed with sewing supplies.

Odd. She always kept her thread tidy, even in a storage closet she hardly used.

Sighing, she shook her head. "Oh, Mr. Boldor, I think I know where you are." Her voice came like a sing-song. She couldn't remember the last time she spoke to a closet, or sang to a door for that matter, but she was giddy as her nerves eased. The danger with Marko had passed. Her dog was unharmed. Her servants were safe.

She stepped over scraps of colorful fabric and entered the closet. Oliver squirmed from her arms and padded on her heels. She heaved the wardrobe to the side and exposed the hidden door leading to the unused servants' quarters in the attic.

Her laugh of disbelief had an edge. "Mr. Boldor, while you

were climbing these stairs to hide, I could've been raped, then killed." She went back into the bedchamber to light a candle, then marched through the sewing closet and clicked open the door leading to the attic. Her dog led her quickly up the stairs.

CHAPTER SEVEN

*P*atience reached the highest step leading to the attic and closed her fingers around the latch. She steeled herself for the sight of Luca. He might be unconscious, his gashes open and bleeding.

If he were alive.

She took a deep breath and flung open the door. A whiff of damp buckskin and green tea filled the air.

Luca was slumped on the floor. Sunlight glinted through a small paned window and the light reflected the shininess of his black hair. Her dog raced ahead and rubbed against Luca's legs, then found a comfortable spot beneath the rafters. She braced one hand on the doorway, the other on the lace at her throat.

"*Kamadiyo.*" His bass voice wove around her as relief turned her legs to silt.

In what appeared a Herculean effort, he pulled himself to sit upright. He was dressed in his breeches and linen shirt, his green sash tied around his waist, his orange scarf folded on his lap.

So engrossed in rushing to him, she didn't stop to

consider her question when she burst out, "Mr. Boldor, how did you climb the stairs with your terrible injuries?"

His face grew so brooding she wondered if he'd heard her.

"I was carried," he finally said.

She set down the candle and took a place on the floor beside him. "Carried by whom?"

Derisive amusement touched his lips. "Penham, I believe, after he found me outside."

"You climbed out the bedchamber window?"

"Aye."

His movements were alarmingly slow and blood from his leg seeped through the tight buckskin. She ran a jerky hand across his knee and felt the stickiness. Her stomach twisted in a thick band of apprehension. "And then?"

"And then I don't remember anything except Penham carrying me up the back stairs, through the guest chamber, and to the attic."

"Many people are carried by God during times of trouble. You were merely carried because of your injuries," she said.

He stretched out his long legs and grimaced. "I'd presumed your attic boasted feathery beds for your servants, but the hard wood floor will have to do."

"This is an unused attic, not a fancy inn."

He laughed, a warm, rich, mellow laugh. "A pity, as I enjoy sliced cottage bread and warm leek stew served on a silver tray in my bedchamber."

She didn't expect his warm laugh nor his wit. He'd seemed so unapproachable. Apparently, his difficult life hadn't vanquished his sense of humor.

"I'm certain your Gypsy tribe furnishes warm meals and feathery beds," she assured.

He shook his head. "You describe your English heaven, not any Romany tribe of mine."

"English and Gypsy heavens are quite similar."

"Gypsies don't go to heaven," he said quietly.

"Of course they do."

Luca's expression darkened, his gaze unwavering. "Did Marko hit your chin?"

The disquiet in his voice was too intense. Patience pulled her gaze from the storminess invading his eyes and focused on her dog sleeping beneath the rafters.

"Aye," she said quietly.

"You shouldn't have suffered on my account."

"The swelling will subside and besides, my injury is naught compared to yours." She eyed the slight bump on the bridge of his nose. Attempting to divert his attention from her chin, she asked, "Did you once break your nose?"

"When I was younger."

"Were you in a brawl?"

"'Tis the injuries done to you"—his voice caught for a moment—"which concern me."

"Mr. Boldor, if we compare injuries, you're the obvious winner."

"This is a contest I prefer neither of us win." Luca tried to rise, appeared to think better of it, and nodded in the direction of the door. "You can assist me down the stairwell."

"Marko is keeping watch. If you want to rest in a lower bedchamber in plain view and place us all at further risk, you'll receive no help from me."

"*Kamadiyo*, you are angry because I ask for assistance?"

She was relieved he was safe. She was relieved he was alive. Nevertheless, with relief came fury at the danger he was in, *they* were in, which he'd brought about by stealing from another tribe.

Her long-suffering composure cracked. "We could've all been killed."

"I will protect you."

She arched a brow. "Really? So far you've done a terrible job. I've protected *you*."

An understanding smile played on his features. "Someday you'll need my protection and I'll be there. However, for now, I need you."

He *needed* her. Even more alarming, his words made her feel safe and reassured, and that all would be well when his wounds healed.

"A brave, protective Gypsy knight isn't a part of any English folklore I remember," she murmured.

"Gypsies are the bravest knights of all, Lady Blakwell. We have nothing to lose, so we have nothing to fear."

She shook her head. "Not when a blackguard like Marko is around."

Luca gripped the black gossamer fabric gathered at her wrists. His mouth knitted into a frown. "I count the days until I can fight Marko."

"I prefer to solve disputes rationally because wrath leads to cruelty. English people solve their disagreements in a civilized fashion."

Imperceptibly, Luca's grip on her sleeve closed tighter. "Say you won't betray me if Marko returns."

"Of course not." She knew her laugh was sardonic. "And I'll do this in exchange for you bursting into my home."

He sat there, ruggedly handsome, yet vulnerable. "You give me more credit than is due," he said. "I didn't burst into your home, I collapsed at your doorstep. Asking for help isn't the usual way of my life."

She jerked her wrist from his grasp. "Indeed, 'tis the only course you seem to know—demanding and demanding more of me each time."

Briefly, she closed her eyes. Somewhere in the mayhem of what she'd once called her emotions, it occurred to her that she'd never been so aware of a man. Her tongue clicked the roof of her mouth, eager to inform Luca that men wreaked havoc in an orderly life, and, for a woman, matrimony was a lifetime sentence. All in trade for security, while a man took whatever he pleased, tiny bits and pieces until a woman was no longer whole. She'd never trust a man again.

She opened her eyes to Luca intently watching her, his dark brows drawn together, offering her an understanding nod.

As before, this indescribable man with the hypnotic voice and horrific injuries made her wonder how he was so perceptive.

"Forgive me, sir. I've endured several difficult weeks since my husband's passing," she said. "He was ill, although a violent thrashing ultimately caused his death and the murderer hasn't been found."

She used Luca's rumpled orange scarf to blot the blood staining his breeches and firmly clamped her lips together. At this rate, she'd become a stuttering henwit who forgot her own name by sunset and spouted inane observations regarding her cruel husband and loveless marriage. And she could sprinkle in her stepson's wrongful accusations, all of which were of little importance to a Gypsy fighting for his life.

Luca halted her agitated fingers and forced her to gaze at him.

"In my tribe, 'tis said that I heal quicker than any man. Some say I am a legend."

She couldn't help but smile, assuming he was trying to lighten her mood. That is, until his voice lowered to a conspiratorial whisper.

"And I heal best in a comfortable feather bed," he said.

Cleverly, he was asserting control, conveniently forgetting he required *her* assistance to reach that very same feather bed.

She dropped the blood-stained scarf on his leg. "If you're not satisfied with the Blakwell lodgings, feel free to sprout wings and go elsewhere."

"Perhaps I should fly away like a pigeon."

She plucked the unlit candle beside her and stood. "Godspeed. Have a safe journey."

The space between them grew silent. A shadow of doubt crossed his features. "Lady Blakwell, why did you lead Marko directly to my bedchamber, thinking I was helpless?"

Coupled with his brusque tone, his eyes had turned as cool and dark as a winter stream.

"You interrogate me like I'm a common criminal. You were safely hidden in the attic by the time Marko and his band of criminals *found* your bedchamber. You obviously didn't hear what went on because you were outside with Penham, but your friend is impossible to deter."

"Marko's not my friend and I instructed you to lie about my whereabouts."

"Mr. Boldor, I did lie. I didn't want to, but I did, in order to protect you."

"And what does your God say to that kind of lie?" Luca asked.

She faltered for a moment. "Matthew in the New Testament says to show forgiveness and store up treasures in heaven."

They fell into quiet. After a few moments, Luca said softly, "Gypsies don't go to heaven, remember?"

"Of course they do."

She watched his chest rise and fall, the hesitancy and flash of hope in his face before he shook his head. "I'll leave tonight," he said.

She rewarded his objection with feigned indifference. "Stay. Go. I shan't take the blame when you collapse in the middle of the stairwell." Half to herself, she muttered,

"Of all the homes in Ipswich, why did you choose this one?"

"Believe me, the home of a *gadje* was the last place I wanted to be."

"I'm almost afraid to ask the meaning of the word."

"A stranger to the Roma. A person who's not one of us."

Their gazes met—his escorted by a grudging smile, edging her to grin. The absurd notion of their conversation and his blunt response surrendered any hope of a serious quarrel.

She laughed outright. "Then we're in complete agreement. You don't want to be here, and I don't want you here. But assuming you're staying, I'll send Penham, my trusted servant, to help you attend to your personal needs in the bath adjacent to the bedchamber below. Then please, please, please return to the attic."

"Aye, but only because you beg so prettily."

With an exasperated shake of her head, she added, "My dog can stay with you. I'll check on my other servants, who surely must think I've forgotten them. Later, I'll send Penham up with a loaf of bread and some nutmeg pudding. In the meantime, don't venture far."

Luca bestowed a mockery of a bow. "For tonight. I'm your submissive patient."

She refused to throw her hands up in frustration, nor deign to reply. Quickly, she quit the attic and descended the stairs. Halfway past her sewing closet, she sniffed and hesitated. Surely the servants hadn't roasted the salted deer without her consent. She'd hoarded the meat for the remaining sparse winter weeks ahead.

She clutched the neckline of her black frock and hastened her steps. Acrid smoke assaulted her nostrils. Dread tingled up her spine. She kept walking, quicker now.

Her disjointed thoughts broke into fragments.

Fire!

The realization wrenched the bottom from her stomach. She dropped the unlit candle, leaving it in pieces on the floor. Her legs raced of their own accord. Reaching the guest bedchamber, she ran to the window and wrenched it open.

Her gasp of shock swept the rooftops. A cloud of smoky blackness blew perilously near the house. Her servants scurried through the snow covered grounds toward the stables.

Patience curled her fingers around the windowpane. Her first cry of panicked denial closed her throat. She dashed through the bedchamber and descended the stairs two at a time. As her feet touched the bottom stair, a low groan told her to glance back.

At the top of the stairs, Luca gripped the balustrade and locked his gaze with hers.

"Why are you running?" he asked.

She tried, but the answer wouldn't come. She was too afraid.

CHAPTER EIGHT

*P*atience allowed Luca's question to hover in the stairway between them.

She reached the entry and Penham was upon her, his arms gesturing wildly. "My lady, the Gypsies set fire to an abandoned stable. Marko shouted that he wanted gold coins for his trouble and that he'd return."

She hardly heard her butler. She nabbed her wool pelisse and bonnet by the door, stepped into her overshoes, and pulled on her gloves. She hurried outside, doubling her strides.

"When did the fire begin?" she asked.

"A short while ago. I crept to the drawing room window, saw Marko torch the stable roof, and heard his threats. The stable boys doused the blaze," Penham said.

"Marko lit the fire to frighten us." She shaded her eyes from the late afternoon sun and peered through the steeple of her hands. A vaporous stream of smoke thickened the sky. A dozen geese flapped their wings, walking and honking across the lawn, their slickly rounded bodies herded together in an effort to escape the confusion.

She headed nearer the smoldering stable. Several yards away, heat forced her footsteps to flag and she blinked and wiped her stinging eyes. In the smudged air, a myriad of servants heaved buckets of water into the dying embers of the burned down stable. Digby mopped the cinders from his forehead and considered her with chilled features.

Lifting her chin, she ignored Digby and asked Penham, "Is anyone injured?"

"Nay, my lady."

"Thank the good Lord for keeping everyone safe." To be heard above the din of splashing water and panicked shouts, she spoke in a loud, calm voice and addressed her servants. "The fire caused little damage and we English don't scare easily." She pushed closer. "I'm confident the Gypsy men are gone."

Her reassurances rang in the scorched air, reassurances even she, the one uttering them, didn't accept as true.

Apparently intent on reading her thoughts, Penham chimed, "Although I fear they'll soon return."

The best response to an alarming statement was no response at all. Saying nothing, Patience regarded a fat hedgehog prowling through the bushes.

Another servant, a young housemaid, called out in a voice as earsplitting as the Ipswich town crier. "Lady Blakwell, where's the injured Gypsy man you took in this morn?"

Patience fingered the fox fur trim at the neckline of her pelisse. Her overshoes sloshed in puddles of snow, and she walked four more paces before coming to a standstill.

Shouting back 'What Gypsy man?' would hardly do. She treated her servants with respect and answered their questions honestly, although the direction of this question was unacceptable. She couldn't tell this housemaid the truth because the housemaid was loyal to Patience's stepson, Crispin.

Patience whirled to the young housemaid and planted her hands on her hips. "The Gypsy man departed. His injuries weren't as severe as I thought and I sent him on his way."

She glanced at Penham. He scuffed the charred ashes in the snow with the toe of his boot and wouldn't meet her gaze.

Patience shook her head. All she did since meeting Luca was lie for him.

She walked over to Penham. With a good-natured smile, she whispered, "I'm thankful for your allegiance."

"'Tis my pleasure, my lady." Penham met her smile with a slow, toothless grin, reminding her that he was an elderly servant, in service to her for many years, and could keep a secret.

❧

*F*or the next several hours, Patience performed her role as dowager countess to a fault.

Admirably. Calmly. Efficiently. Nonetheless, she glanced up the stairwell each time she passed, imagining a pale and weak Luca standing there.

When a supper of capon, beets, and a small salad ended at seven o'clock, Amelia, Patience's lady's maid, flung open the entry door. With a flourish, she deposited her traveling trunk in the hall.

"Here I am," Amelia declared, as if she were the Regent King of England waiting for his subjects to applaud, rather than a servant to a soon-to-be destitute dowager duchess. Amelia hung her pelisse by the doorway, shook her black muslin skirt, and spread open her ample arms. "I returned a day earlier than planned. From the looks of the rubble in the field, I'm back just on time." She frowned. "My lady, your lip is swollen and your chin is bruised."

Patience rushed to her maid's side and extended Amelia a

sincere hug of affection. She regarded Amelia as her only family, her personal lady's maid. Neither young nor French, as was the custom, Amelia was old and proper and English. Opinionated, aye, but kind-hearted and faithful in her walk with the Lord.

"'Tis nothing," Patience said. "How fares your uncle in Bucklesham?"

"He's as tight as a drum, foxed as usual, and refused to provide so much as a spare shilling to help you."

"My dearest maid, thank you for trying to help."

"Can you contact your cousin, Faith, in Whitehaven to help?" Amelia asked. "She and her older sister and brother are said to live prosperously."

"I haven't corresponded with them in years, and heard there was a scandal in their family recently. They never answer my letters."

Amelia's voice fell to a whisper. "Surely your stepson cannot charge you with such a terrible sin as murder without proof, my lady?"

"I have faith that my stepson will eventually give up this nonsense. I was a devoted wife to my late husband and no one can claim otherwise."

Amelia shot a look around the empty hall. "You endured more cruelty than any young woman should bear in one lifetime."

Heat crawled up Patience's cheeks. She stepped back. "You knew? What my husband did? When we were alone?" The humiliating intimacies increased tenfold by the knowl-edge that her maid had been aware of what had happened. Every night of Patience's loveless marriage she'd breathed the same vinegary sourness on her late husband's sweat-stained pillow.

She shivered and wrapped her arms around herself. She could still feel his gold rings bearing down on her shoulders.

"Most of the servants knew that Lord Blakwell was a vile man." Amelia extracted a white, embroidered linen handkerchief from her sleeve and dabbed at her eyes. Then she stuffed her handkerchief in her bodice and glanced at the door. "Smoke lingers in the fields. Servants are creeping about and whispering of an injured Gypsy disappearing out the window." Amelia's gaze quickened to the housemaids entering the dining room and clearing the dinner dishes, wiping their hands on their white, ruffled aprons. They set hazelnuts, grapes, and walnuts in a silver bowl on a mahogany side table.

"Did I miss the meal?" Amelia asked.

"Before you eat," Patience said, "I must speak with you in private first." Effectively silencing her maid's habit to prattle on without a breath, she guided Amelia to the drawing room. They settled on a settee near the bay window and pianoforte. Patience kept a firm watch to ensure no servants wandered near.

"Gypsies attacked this morn and set fire to an abandoned stable," she said.

Amelia yanked the handkerchief from her bodice and clapped it to her lips. Her eyes widened like two hazel orbs. "I heard tales of a tribe of Gypsies camped by the river near Ipswich. Why would they come to your dower house? We're far removed here in the country."

"These particular Gypsies seek a man."

"Gypsies roam all the time, and with all that wandering, they shouldn't be surprised to lose a man every so often."

Patience extracted the handkerchief from her maid's hand and waved it like a matador to attract her attention. "They're desperately serious to find him."

"Desperate Gypsies steal and pillage." Amelia's amiable face changed from one of worry to one reddened with conviction. "We should notify the law, the constable, the Prince Regent!"

She placed the handkerchief back in Amelia's hands.

"No law is forceful enough to outmaneuver a cold-blooded man like Marko. He and his tribe intended to kill the man they were seeking, as well as anyone who kept him hidden."

"Thank our gracious God this isn't our concern."

Patience focused on Amelia's adamant tilt of her head and the silver wisps of hair escaping from her mob cap. Like Penham, Patience knew she could trust Amelia. Both servants were with her before she'd married her husband, whereas the other servants had been hired afterward by her husband.

Patience squeezed Amelia's hands to soften the next bit of information. "The Gypsy man they seek is convalescing in our attic. I hid him there."

Amelia's handkerchief slipped silently to the floor.

Fearing she'd reduced her maid to speechlessness, a state she'd never seen her in before, Patience relied on Amelia's Christian spirit to overcome her objections.

"He's severely injured and in pain," Patience said. "I need your help to care for him properly and secretly. Within a fort-night, he'll be mended and on his way."

Amelia's brows puckered.

Patience stood before her maid voiced any protests. "Come and meet him."

~

A reassuring peek in Luca's empty bedchamber prompted Patience's heart to skip in relief. He'd actually listened to her advice. With a half-smile, she tugged Amelia through the sewing closet and up the stairs to the attic.

Patience was aware of him before she saw him. He dozed in a corner beneath the eaves, his stained orange scarf draped around him. His face, like bronzed satin, absorbed the winks of moonlight peeking through the tiny, paned window. The muscles in his arms bunched as he leaned on one elbow. His long legs sprawled lengthwise, his worn leather boots set haphazardly beside him.

Patience latched the attic door shut without a sound.

He jerked up. Quicker than a panther, he unsheathed a dagger from his boot and raised the shiny blade.

Amelia shrieked.

Patience stepped in front of the maid. "Mr. Boldor, what are you doing?"

Slowly, he lowered his hand. His wrist shook. He was still so weak.

He sat heavily against the wall and frowned. "'Tis a habit to always be on guard for an unwelcome visitor."

"I live here, remember? And whom did you expect—a night watchman? Put the dagger away." Patience extended her hand. "Better yet, give it to me."

"This I cannot do." He sheathed the dagger and slipped it into his boot. His well-muscled body, though injured, conveyed authority, like the fighter he surely was. A life spent living outdoors had hard-edged his features and creased his forehead into tiny lines.

"I trust the fire from earlier this afternoon was doused?" he asked.

"Aye, although the stable is reduced to ashes. Marko must have a brother named Hades."

She expected Luca to smile at her jest. He didn't.

"When I'm strong, I'll right the injustices done to you today," he said solemnly.

"Please, no violence. Thank the good Lord no one was harmed."

"If it were not for my injuries I would have—"

"You would've jeopardized everyone on the Blakwell

estate if you'd stormed onto the fields with a bucket of water in your hands," Patience said.

He smiled, and his jaw lost some of its stiffness. He glanced in Amelia's direction, as if he'd noticed her for the first time.

"Who's she?"

"My personal maid, Amelia. She's a very patient caregiver."

Ignoring Amelia entirely, Luca stared at Patience, his black eyebrows in two upraised arches. "You will not care for me, *kamadiyo*? Do you leave all the difficult tasks to servants?" His voice matched his expression, both bland, as if his opinion of her had lessened.

She prickled. "I sewed your wounds and washed your gashes, remember? And tended to you since you've arrived. You're the one who should be chastised. Amelia is a trusted servant and most compassionate."

Never at a loss for words before, Patience's indignant maid stood surprisingly thunderstruck. Indelicately, the maid coughed several times into her handkerchief while blasting glower after glower at Luca as she waddled toward him.

Patience's dog cocked his head and considered Amelia's coughing spasm with a lid twitch.

Luca bestowed on her maid the most charismatic smile Patience had ever seen. "My lovely Amelia, you woke Lady Blakwell's dog, if not the entire household, with your raspy cough," he said. "Consider downing a generous cup or two of stinging nettles...to loosen the cough."

Her maid rent him a critical glare. "Mr. Gypsy, if you're such an expert on sickness, then you can easily look after yourself." Apparently reunited with her voice, she added, "Because I refuse to attend to a dagger-wielding savage!"

Patience closed her eyes and hoped, when she opened them, that Luca might have dozed off, or Amelia might have disappeared. She opened her eyes to find Amelia with her mouth open in poised position, and Luca very much awake.

Meeting Patience's gaze, his mouth lifted so faintly she wondered if the smile was intentional.

"Aye. I see what you mean." His shoulders seemed to shake in silent laughter. "Your maid is most compassionate."

CHAPTER NINE

Fortunately, Patience's stepson, Crispin, lived in London, and her handful of servants, save for Penham and Amelia, didn't know that she hid a Gypsy in the attic. The servants went about their daily duties, then returned to the servants' bedrooms in the basement. Several had worked at the Blakwell house for less than a year, which was typical because servants were fluid. They rose early, stopping when Patience awoke, then completed their tasks in the evening. They were expected to remain out of sight and be silent.

Penham and Amelia slept in separate wings in small garret rooms in the attic. They were elderly, devoted servants and remained supportive of Patient's decision, providing discreet help in caring for Luca.

Still, Patience was a dowager countess, and she knew that many people would surely disapprove. This reasoning, and the attraction she felt whenever she came within two feet of Luca, kept her well away from the attic.

Amelia settled into the daily routine of tending to him. She brought him plates filled with baked eggs on toast, roasted chicken livers, and boiled ham sprinkled with paprika, proclaiming that all Gypsies liked liberal doses of paprika. On several occasions, she and Penham managed to sneak up a metal hip-bath and fresh water for Luca to bathe.

The days progressed, and Amelia grudgingly muttered that Luca proved a most cooperative patient. For a Gypsy, he never got riled. Furthermore, he was extremely courteous, even though she knew he was in terrible pain whenever she rubbed her special liniment into his raw gashes.

Four days after he'd arrived on Patience's doorstep, Amelia whispered to Patience after dinner that Mr. Boldor would be departing the following morn. In an abrupt and astounding gush of apologies for being unable to see him off, the red-faced maid brandished her ever-present handkerchief and bid Patience to wish him a safe journey.

"I have a midnight meeting on the outskirts of Ipswich," Amelia declared between bites of apple tarte, brushing her frock free of the last bit of crumbs. As she hurried from the dining room, she donned her pelisse and secured the frog fastenings.

Patience blinked in confusion, an empty platter arrested in her hands. "What sort of meeting convenes at midnight?"

White streamers askew from her maid's cap, Amelia bustled into the kitchen and out the pantry door. "A meeting of utmost importance."

Patience peered out the bay window of the drawing room just as Amelia bobbled through the moonlit fields. She towed a large travel bag, her pelisse flailing in the night breeze. She'd declined the use of a driver and carriage, preferring to walk.

Walk? On a cold, dark night? Amelia never walked anywhere during the day, let alone at night. Perhaps she'd planned a meeting with a secret gentleman. Patience accompanied that thought with a negative shake of her head. On more than one occasion, she'd witnessed Amelia vocally lashing a suitor whom she'd deemed below her station. And any wealthy aristocrat above her station wouldn't traipse about Ipswich at midnight.

Patience wandered through the rooms of the house, dawdling in the dining room, feigning interest in imagined particles of dust on the rims of each serving piece. All in a futile effort to keep her hands busy and her wits occupied until she bid Luca farewell.

As evening shadows deepened, the servants finished their chores and retired. At nine o'clock, a housemaid went to Patience's bedchamber to draw the heavy curtains and set a cup of tea on Patience's nightstand. After the housemaid left, Patience hurried to the kitchen and wrapped several green apples and a slab of brown bread in a knapsack. With one last guarded look over her shoulders, she hid the knapsack beneath her paisley shawl and climbed the stairs.

She stopped in her second floor bedchamber to unfasten her mob cap and release her waist-length hair. Comb in hand, she pulled her hair up so tightly her eyes watered, then secured the crown with a plain white ribbon. She sipped her tea and stared at herself in the mirror. Hardly widow-like, her auburn hair curled in ringlets below her shoulders.

She reached the attic stairs with her knapsack and reminded herself of how relieved she'd be when Luca was gone. Amelia's opinion might've wavered, but Patience worried that beneath Luca's rugged appeal was a practiced rogue, a vagabond at best.

But there was another reason why she wanted him gone. There was a connection between them that was unexplainable and disconcerting. Her brain warned avoidance, but a quiet nagging in her heart encouraged her to confront her emotions.

So here she stood, on the top step leading to the attic.

Taking a deep breath, she knocked once on the door and entered.

Luca sat beneath the paned glass attic window with his legs drawn to his chest. He was fully dressed in his linen shirt and buckskin breeches. His worn leather pouch hung at his side. The air smelled of him, dark peppery spices and leather.

He clutched a quill pen and scratched on a piece of paper perched on his knees. When their gazes joined, his eyes reflected a mischievous smile. He raised the quill pen. "You caught me."

"'Tis hardly a crime to hold a pen."

From the questioning look on his face, she assumed he wanted an explanation for her unannounced visit.

"Amelia said you're to depart in the morning," she said. "I came to bid you a safe journey." She eyed the pen inquisitively, then him. "There are no signs of Marko and you look well. Have you given any thought to leaving tonight instead of tomorrow?"

Luca set the quill on the paper and rubbed a thumb across his unshaven chin. "A splendid idea. You shall finally be rid of me."

Patience walked to several stools stacked against the wall and retrieved his cloak and cravat. "You purposely misunderstood me." She came toward him, closing the distance, then lurched back at the resentment leaping from his eyes. He truly was the most proud, overconfident man she'd ever met.

"I worry for your safety," she admitted quietly. "You're not that strong, although I know you're anxious to return to your tribe."

Luca picked up the quill again, scraping ink against paper, thoroughly ignoring her.

Taking his silence as acquiescence, she motioned to the quill. "You have a long journey ahead of you knowing that

Marko is skulking about, yet you while away your last hours of safety by sketching?"

Ink against paper. Ink against paper. Scraping. Scratching. Rubbing.

"Mr. Boldor?" She held his cloak out to him. "Are you fit to travel this evening? You'd be better escaping detection at night."

The seconds of silence ticked while she watched his closed expression. He squeezed the tip of the quill and his strokes came swift and firm.

Unhurriedly, he lifted his head. "Where do you imagine I travel, Lady Blakwell?" he asked silkily. "Perhaps a filthy camp by a nameless river?"

"I don't judge you by where or how you live."

His earlier smile faded, the spark in his eyes snuffed out. "You performed your honor-bound deed and saved a poor, homeless beggar. Your conscience should be clear."

"Amelia is a fine caregiver."

"And I heal quickly."

She heard the underlying resentment in his tone, and without understanding why, felt deflated. Under his fixed stare, she shifted his cloak from one arm to the other and fingered a patch of rabbit fur haphazardly sewn on the sleeve.

"I didn't realize Gypsies could write," she said.

A muscle twitched in his jaw. "Do you assume all Roma are illiterate?"

Her breath wedged in her throat and she forced out a 'nay.' "You rummaged through numerous trunks in the attic to search not for a traveling bag, nor a spare blanket for your journey, but a quill pen?" she asked.

"I carry my pen and paper with me."

He carried a quill pen. And paper. And a silver dagger.

A Gypsy, a nomad, a man who wasn't supposed to be able to read, much less write.

She gestured to the paned window. "Why did you move to the other side of the attic? Is the light better?"

He set the quill and paper on the floor. "I refuse to sit facing a portrait of a dead man. 'Tis unsettling." Luca motioned to a dusty painting hung crooked on a far wall.

Lord Bertram Blakwell.

The colors had faded with time, but the crafty blue eyes and distinguished white beard still managed to make her feel afraid and chilled and sick to her stomach.

"I doubt any man, dead or alive, could unsettle you," she said.

"'Tis your late husband."

"How did you know?" she asked.

"I read as well as write. Lord Blakwell's name is clearly etched in the corner of the frame."

Her glance fell to the portrait and back to Luca. In a vigilant attempt to change the subject, she asked the first question springing to her tongue. "Why are you using a quill?"

"Perhaps I'm writing a letter to my tribe to ask how they're faring without my protection. That is, if I can string five words into a sentence." Luca waited a long time before continuing. "In my letter, I'll ask the elders if I should trust you, an Englishwoman, and journey tonight. Or, should I wait until morn as Amelia suggested? Is your eagerness for my departure a deathtrap in disguise?"

Patience dropped his cloak at his feet. "If I wished this, wouldn't I have refused to help you when I first found you in my home? And I didn't mean to belittle you nor your people."

"Perhaps not intentionally."

She heard his irritation. He'd remembered their conversation, despite his pain, despite his feverish moans. And because she'd been preoccupied with tending to him, he'd assumed she'd been disinterested in his ways and his tribe.

"Some Englishmen believe that Gypsies are uneducated. Be assured these are not my beliefs," was all she said.

"The Rom are savages, if I remember correctly."

"Amelia's words," Patience corrected.

"Whereas the English are—what was the word you used— aye, of course. The English are gentlemen."

"Civilized," she said.

Unable to contain her curiosity, she bent to view the paper and her gaze froze midway between awe and incredulity. No black marks were illegibly scrawled. The likeness staring back at her mirrored familiarity and such lovely features that she caught her breath.

"This woman's face is so serene, so life-like."

"'Tis you."

She jerked to her feet and retreated. "Me? I'm not this woman. She's young, perhaps sixteen years old. I'm one and twenty, soundly past the age of a maid, although I recall my sixteenth year clearly." She hesitated, terrible memories roiling through her. "'Tis the year I married Lord Blakwell."

"A young girl betrothed to an old man."

Self-respect made her stand taller. "I had no choice."

"A hard-hearted choice, if we tallied your English ways compared to the Rom. Is marriage to a wealthy old man perfectly respectable for a young English lady?"

"I wed whomever my father chose because my marriage protected the decent name of my parents and ensured their welfare."

Luca's mouth downturned. He shook his head.

"People have sanctioned arranged marriages for centuries," she said.

"An impressive speech, Lady Blakwell, but most ineffective." He pushed to his feet while he tied the green sash around his waist and fetched his cloak and paper off the floor.

"And from the dueling swords your pretty eyes flash, shall we consider this conversation a draw?"

"You're not above reproach," she said. "You told a falsehood by allowing me to think you were writing a letter."

"You came to your own conclusions."

She glanced at the paper, at the wide blue eyes of her youth, shining with excitement. "Your sketch isn't a true depiction of me."

"I sketched what I saw. You display such sweet innocence."

Briefly, she closed her eyes. "I'm a widow and anything but innocent. If you wish to compliment me, you do a poor job. In any case, I'm immune to compliments."

He genuinely smiled. "All women enjoy compliments, Lady Blakwell."

"And because I'm a widow, you assume I'm ripe to your trickery and silver tongue."

"I'm a Roma. You describe my specialty."

She shook her head. "No woman in her right mind would ever fancy your flowery words."

He placed one hand to his chest. "You're breaking your patient's heart."

"Better than your leg."

Despite their attempt to make light of his grim situation and imminent departure, the mood sobered and her heart gave a funny lurch.

He came nearer, reminding her of his overpowering height. In one hand he held his cloak and pouch, carelessly thrown over his shoulder. In the other, he clutched the paper. He suppressed a groan when he put weight on his leg, and she grabbed his forearms before he could take another step.

"Mr. Boldor, wait and leave in the morning. I'm sorry that I suggested you leave tonight. Each day you'll grow stronger," she said.

"I'm accustomed to the pain in my leg." With scrupulous politeness, he extended the sketch to her. "Please accept this humble gift for saving my life."

She released her grip, stepped back, and ran a hand along her gown. "I cannot accept a gift so personal."

He cupped her hands and urged the crinkled paper into her palms. "I'm indebted and want to repay you, as 'tis the way of the Rom. Close your fingers around my sketch and say *'nais tuke.'* Thank you."

She couldn't. She wouldn't. She'd be vulnerable if she accepted such a personal gift, and vulnerability frightened her, because she'd become weak and defenseless. She couldn't trust that a man would only want to thank her with a small gift, even if his demeanor and mannerisms were kind and thoughtful. He'd want more.

She rolled the paper between her fingers and shook her head in refusal. "Nay."

"Wrong word and wrong gesture." Luca took her hands and folded them around the paper. "I will not leave until you grant me the favor of accepting my gift."

Perhaps it was his sincerity that kept her fingers gripped around the paper. Or perhaps it was the earnestness in his dark eyes.

"Grant me the favor of accepting my gift. And say *'nais tuke'* in return, *kamadiyo.*"

Her gaze drifted to his firm lips. A pale hidden smile reminded her that many women's heartbeats might flutter around him, but she wouldn't permit hers to be one of them.

"*Kamadiyo,*" she said quietly. "Your mysterious word with no meaning."

"Aye." The engaging, utterly charming grin he gave triumphed over her misgivings. He knew it would. Just as he knew his voice was so compelling that she'd forget her own name if he kept speaking.

The sketch was a simple gift with neither obligation nor hidden meaning. A gift meant acceptance and appreciation, as wondrous as a new cloth doll had once been at Christmas. She needed to give him nothing in return. He was simply expressing his appreciation.

Clasping the paper, she murmured, "Very well. Thank you."

"*Nais tuke*," he reminded.

"*Nais tuke*."

He dropped his cloak and pouch and gazed at her. "When last I saw you, your lip was swollen from Marko's cruel hand." He lifted his fingers. "May I?"

She nodded. "Aye."

Lightly, he traced her lips. "The swelling is gone."

"Because I heal quickly," she said.

"Then we have much in common." Bending his head, he brushed his lips across hers. She closed her eyes and heard her own sudden intake of breath. *Stop this madness* some part of her implored, but not the part she listened to. Logic reeled. This man was neither a barbarian nor a savage. He was a gifted artist.

"This was not part of our arrangement," he said in an undertone, as if arguing with himself.

He placed his arms around her shoulders, holding her as gently as a precious jewel. Yet memories of her late husband's hands pitiless groping made her jerk back.

Luca dropped his hands. His thumbs moved to her shoulders, tenderly, carefully, pushing down her panic.

She shook her head. "My life has no room for this."

"Make room." He nestled her close to his chest and her cheeks rubbed against the cool linen of his shirt. Near him, she knew exhilaration and peacefulness, two differing ends of an unbending spectrum.

His clear gaze probed hers. He was seeking something,

and, while seeking, he threatened to usurp every secure boundary she'd carefully erected around her heart. And when he tired of her, he'd leave with nary a backward glance.

She leaned her head back and offered an intentionally careless smile. "Have you discovered a new technique to aid your healing? Sketching your caretaker and then kissing her?"

"I believe that you are my true caregiver. The urge to sketch and kiss Amelia never occurred to me."

Her disloyal pulse quickened to triple time. "Amelia mentioned you ate heartily these past few days. You have a large appetite if my empty pantry is any indication."

"Amelia is a veritable chatterbox who never takes a breath," he said dryly. "She doles out an opinion on every subject that ever graced England's shores."

He glanced toward the window and frowned.

Patience slipped from him and reached for the knapsack. "I brought you a slab of bread and some apples for your journey."

He cast a quick appraisal at the fare, then back at the window. "You were right. I must go tonight. I've stayed too long and I don't belong here. This is an English world." Still frowning, Luca picked up his cloak and swung the pouch over his shoulder. "I'll use the back stairwell. Once I reach the woods, I'll follow the river. Amelia explained the route in excruciating detail and I didn't have the heart to tell her that the Rom have traveled these paths for centuries."

Patience searched his handsome face, now disengaged and preoccupied. He was leaving and the realization hit in a rush. The razor thin stillness was punctuated with no explanations. Effectively, he'd sliced a clean division.

"It's probably better to leave when it's dark, after all. Goodbye, Mr. Boldor."

"Good night, Lady Blakwell. I'll keep watch and listen for information regarding Marko's whereabouts while I travel. If

I hear he's headed back here, I'll return. I assure you that you'll be safe." Luca turned on his heels and left her standing in the middle of the attic.

Without preamble, he reached for the latch, then closed the door behind him.

She clutched his sketch in one hand and the knapsack in the other. He'd forgotten the food. She stared at the door, mindful of the dull ache compressing her chest, the heavy loneliness constricting her breath.

Wind scoured through the cracks in the rafters, bringing a whiff of peppery spices. Somewhere outside, footsteps crunched through the snow and a tree limb snapped. She held the knapsack close and found her control hidden beneath a choked swallow. No tears, of course. Only a heavy, nagging ache in the hollow of her chest. He'd bid her good night as if nothing significant had occurred between them. And he'd left with nary a backward glance.

CHAPTER TEN

*L*uca glared in mounting irritation at the tall, broad-shouldered lad in yellow breeches scampering far ahead. He'd discovered Pulko behind a tree almost immediately after departing Lady Blakwell's house.

Normally, Pulko never outran Luca. Now, Luca's leg allowed him no more than a sluggish limp through an icy, moonlit countryside while he trailed a boy half his age.

Pulko wielded a sackful of food and seldom glanced over his shoulder. Before sunrise, he slowed and doubled back across the fields. "I see some tents," he called out. "We're almost home. Hurry."

With each labored step, Luca's thoughts grew stormier, especially when Pulko feigned absorption in the brightening sky instead of Luca's uneven gait. Luca clamped his teeth together and hoped the throbbing in his leg ceased once he'd reached his familiar tent.

"Have you decided to allow me an extra minute to catch up?" he asked.

The boy peered dully over his shoulder. He heaved his sack to the ground and plopped himself on top. "You cannot help your slowness. You tire easily because of Marko's thrashing."

"Very understanding," Luca said sardonically. He pulled his attention from his discomfort to the questions burning at him throughout their journey. Trying to keep his manner non-critical, he studied Pulko's impish face, the black straggles of Pulko's mustache, and weighed his words. "Why did you reappear at Lady Blakwell's house hours earlier than I expected? Amelia told me you weren't due back until early morn, after she met you by the river with supplies for our tribe."

The boy shrugged. "The tribe required more food. I raided the countess's kitchen pantry one last time."

"By climbing onto the rooftop of her house? I looked out the window and expected to see the sky, not a flash of a blue cloak. The roof is steeply pitched and you could've fallen. If you expect me to commend you, 'twill be for your foolishness, not your daring. And if you expect me to believe you, I'm disappointed you think me such a fool."

Pulko swung his legs down from the sack. "I stood on the roof of Lady Blakwell's house to be sure that Marko wasn't about."

"I don't need a young scoundrel to look out for me. I take care of myself."

"Marko's out for vengeance. He'll find you. 'Tis rumored he's still in Ipswich," Pulko said.

Luca considered Pulko's words. There'd been no sign of Marko, but Lady Blakwell would be vulnerable and in danger if Marko was still sniffing around Ipswich.

He sighed and rubbed his face. His tribe had been waiting several days for his return. They needed to break camp and head for the coast. They'd exhausted their food and supplies, and he couldn't leave them in the hands of young Pulko without checking on them.

He eyed Pulko's mop of dark hair, the heavy, dark brows

offset by a roguish grin. Although Pulko's voice had deepened and his chest and arms had filled out within the past year, Luca still considered Pulko a child.

Aloud, Luca said, "We must break camp and journey toward the sea immediately."

Pulko's face brightened. "An excellent idea because the tribe grows tired of Ipswich and Portman's meadow. The farmers are wary of us and there's little left to pilfer. The elders say you lead us back to Ipswich every year because your English father might still live here. Why don't you confront him and tell him who you are?"

"My father's a cruel man. He deserted me and my mother and he's dead to me." The words stung as Luca uttered them. He released a deep breath. His father wasn't a part of his life anymore and Luca had been raised by a kind, caring tribe, which was more than enough for any man.

From sheer habit, Luca scanned the forest bordering the riverbank, looking for enemy Rom or English intent on harming Gypsies. Daylight spilled across the field, glistening the frost to shiny white dust and showing no foreign footprints.

Luca crooked his index finger and beckoned Pulko nearer. "So then, why were you spying on me while I bid goodbye to Lady Blakwell?"

The boy rose taller, almost to the height of Luca's shoulders. "We depend on you, and you stayed in the English-woman's house far too many days."

"I was recuperating, and this matter isn't for you to decide."

"You were with a *gadje,* a stranger. *Gadje Gadjensa, Rom Romensa. Gadje* should stay with *Gadje*, *Rom* with *Rom*."

"My mother once said that I resembled my English father more than a Rom." Luca's words were disjointed, as if stuck in another place.

"Some of the elders said that she spoke highly of your father," Pulko said.

Something, Luca added to himself, he never intended to do. The familiar aloofness closed his heart and a long-forgotten memory flicked across his mind. His beautiful, dark-haired mother standing near their tent, cupping a tiny finch in her hand, laughing softly when the bird sang. Remembering his mother added to his loathing for the absent nobleman who'd used her, then cast her and their young son off when he grew disinterested. She'd died heartbroken and alone.

And then there were whispers of Luca's twin brother, a baby who'd died at birth. Some tribesmen had mentioned the baby's death was a result of Luca being born too strong and rebellious, taking all the air in his mother's womb, whereas his brother was born stillborn, too frail to survive.

Quelling the ever-present guilt, Luca nodded curtly at Pulko. "Lady Blakwell's maid, Amelia, is a *gadje*. You seemed to get along well with her."

"She gave me food. I didn't venture too close, though, or she would've contaminated me." Pulko lowered his voice to a conspiratorial whisper. "I saw you kiss Lady Blakwell. You're definitely contaminated."

"So you *were* spying on me. When you grow older, you'll want to kiss a woman, especially a beautiful woman."

Pulko reached into the sack, pulled off a fistful of bread, and stuffed it in his mouth. "Girls are needy nuisances."

"I taught you well, but some women are virtuous and brave."

Like Lady Blakwell. She'd deterred Marko single-handedly. A rare woman indeed, she'd managed to squeeze Luca's cynical heart with an affection he hadn't known existed. She spoke of Christian ways, of kindness, and consideration, and a true caring for others.

He closed his eyes to focus on her skeptical smile when he'd told her she was sweet and innocent.

'I'm a widow and anything but innocent. If you wish to compliment me, you do a poor job.'

With a noiseless groan, he opened his eyes. Better to expose his heart to his worst enemy than a prim and proper English noblewoman. No matter how kind she was, the English he'd known proved cruel and uncaring.

Luca and Pulko resumed their pace, their strides taking them to the top of the clearing. Hardly visible through the blackthorn trees, a scattering of recognizable *benders*, tents, came into view, along with an assortment of dilapidated brown carts and three-wheeled wagons.

Luca stamped the snow off his boots and stood silent. He cupped his hands and blew into his palms to warm them. There was much to do—greet the elders, ensure everyone had food, and then prepare for the tribe's departure. Afterward, when his tribesmen were settled around a sputtering, smoky campfire, he'd mention Lady Blakwell's courage and kindness.

His mind flashed to how she'd looked before he'd quit the attic—grappling a knapsack for him in one hand, which his pride had refused to accept—and his sketch of her in the other. He visualized her high, wide cheekbones overshadowed by glorious sapphire eyes and curly auburn hair.

He owed her his life, although he'd never see her again. He had a tribe to care for, she had an English society to live in.

Wending his way into camp, he yanked off his orange scarf and waved it high. Diverted by lively howls of delight, he breathed in whiffs of singed game, undiluted wine, and finely ground hot pepper. Amidst welcoming handshakes and relieved embraces, utterances of '*Sar shan,*' and 'how are you', his grin overtook his face.

He was needed. He was where he belonged. He was home.

CHAPTER ELEVEN

*S*tanding near the entryway to his *bender*, tent, Luca shifted and braced for the blast of pain sure to follow. He tried to think of something, anything, to stop the sudden knifelike agony. Only a lovely English woman came to mind, and he focused his thoughts on Patience's delicate face. Behind her tranquil smile, she was a lady with more pluck and honor than a man four times her size. Her valor for saving his life had nearly cost her own.

When he'd kissed her, her formalness had fallen away. She'd tried to suppress her feelings under light quips and lighter banter, despite her lingering smile and softly parted lips.

But now he was back with his needy tribe.

And Marko was angrily stalking about somewhere.

And Patience was alone and unguarded.

Luca's left knee buckled, and he struggled to adjust his weight to his right leg. He leaned heavily on the walking stick he'd devised out of an oak tree branch to keep the pressure off his bad knee. Fourteen days and nights of continuous dampness had prevented his injuries from healing properly.

He viewed the early streaks of daylight, the flicker of intermittent campfires. He sniffed appreciatively, although the tang of moist earth and cloves and wood smoke did little to raise his mood.

Wintry rain coated the branches of blackthorn trees and a faint tinkling of sleet hit the ground. Waterlogged, his tribe's camp stood draped in a soggy mist. Squeaky wagon wheels groaned deeper into a thick sludge of mud and snow. Every day that passed, each drop of icy rain that fell, made attempts to break camp more and more difficult. He glanced at the crude stable and the two dapple-gray horses Pulko had stolen several months earlier. The old horses would have a wretched time lugging the wagons if the sleet and rain continued.

When their tribe left a place, they had nowhere in mind, no place to walk, no place to push their carts. But still they'd walk, still they'd push. And in each new village, Luca hoped his heart would find a home, that this was the place he truly belonged. He winced, a slight heaviness in his stomach. Would his feelings of restlessness never cease?

A fierce split of thunder broke his musings in half, and he shook his head at his inability to control the weather, his tribe's inability to leave, and the vulnerable position Lady Blakwell was placed in on his account.

He closed the flap of his tent and retrieved his cloak and pouch, then limped through a clump of slick leaves to Pulko's *bender*. For balance, Luca depended more and more on his walking stick. He hated the wretched thing.

As Luca approached, Pulko poked his head from the opening of his canvas tent. "Are we leaving for Colchester today?"

"Unfortunately, the miserable weather fails to cooperate."

The canvas flapped open and Pulko's mother, Fabiana, emerged. At a height close to Luca's, she faced him eye to eye. The center of her black gaze gleamed like a new pair of leather boots.

"How's your leg?" she asked.

There was little use in lying to a woman who knew him better than a son.

"The pain has worsened," he admitted. Intent on the icy rain cooling his overheated flesh, he raised his cloak, and showed them his wound. He'd slit the leg of his breeches so he could roll up the pant leg.

"*Prikaza.* Your luck is bad because your wound is taking so long to heal, although the stitching looks neat and clean." Fabiana knotted her bright pink shawl around her shoulders and clucked. "I'm impressed at the good care you got from a *mahrime*, an unclean and impure English woman."

"She gave me excellent care." Luca clarified as he draped his ragged woolen cloak closer about himself. He glanced toward Fabiana's tent. "Perhaps a cup of hot tea will help ease the soreness in my leg."

"No tea, only water from the stream. You're not in a rich English manor anymore with a cook and steward." With a hmph, Fabiana reentered her *bender* and poured the water from a jug, handing the cup to Luca.

Luca smiled as he accepted. He drank, then lowered the cup, circling the rim with his fingers. He glimpsed one of the elderly Rom's campfire through a patch of woods and walked toward it, crossing a stream and rotted wooden fence.

Several large open wagons piled with clothes and trinkets stood beneath a covering of trees. Shaky carts missing several wheels, creaked with the wind. Two thin, dark-eyed children swung upside down on a crude hammock tied to the trees. They smiled and waved as he passed. He bent and playfully mussed their hair, then reached into his cloak and offered them an apple to share.

A group of older women danced on a cracked barn door

that they'd used for a floor, swaying their large hips in time to rattling tambourines and ascending modes.

Four of the elders seated around the campfire studied Luca with narrowed eyes as he approached. The gaiety ceased. The music stopped. All the tribesmen, Luca's tribesmen, were wary of his association with Lady Blakwell, the Englishwoman, despite the fact that she'd helped him.

One of the elderly men, Besnik, stood as Luca approached. His worn-down face boasted shriveled cheeks and no brows. "Pulko said we're to break camp and leave Portman's meadow."

"As soon as the weather cooperates," Luca replied. "Our tribe will find food by the sea."

"Will living by the sea keep us safe from Marko's men who want vengeance, or from the English who hate us?" Besnik pressed. "Or shall we assume the English are now our friends?"

A lean dog sniffed at Luca's heels as he knelt by the campfire and warmed his hands. Flimsy tents rocked in the slight breeze, as if sensing his tribe's unrest.

"Lady Blakwell showed me that not all English are as cruel as I believed," he said.

The men didn't seem persuaded. Their faces remained impassive. Silently, they shared a jug of brandy and wiped their mouths on their sleeves after each guzzle.

Luca stood. "May I join you?"

They shrugged and made room for him on a spongy log.

Luca refused the brandy jug as it was refilled and passed, smiling politely. Though few in number, these were his people, and they needed him as their leader. Proud, enterprising, and self-sufficient, they worked at whatever tasks were available to them, selling fruit and mending bellows, weaving baskets and harvesting crops.

His thoughts moved to Lady Blakwell. Aye, she employed

servants, yet he worried for her safety. She couldn't protect herself against the likes of Marko and his men.

He sighed, deeply. He was only one man and couldn't be in two places at the same time.

He belonged here in the forest by a campfire, not in her upper-class, stiff English dining room. Besides, she deserved an upright, honest, and wealthy Englishman as her protector, not a dark-colored thief.

He sat quiet, reflecting. He and Patience were so different. He'd lied his way through life in order to ensure his tribe didn't starve. What would she think if she knew his past, the brawls too numerous to count, the stolen chickens numbering in the hundreds, the clothes and jewelry and coins pilfered from purses of unsuspecting noblemen?

Misha, one of the crinkly bearded elders, brought Luca back to the present with his bellowing voice. "Nadya is marrying a lord of one of the richer tribes. She's through dallying with Marko, and with you, too, apparently."

"My tryst with Nadya ended a long time ago," Luca clarified. "I wish her much happiness."

"She'll marry the rich lord for his money." Misha took another swill of brandy.

Gazing at the campfire, Luca said, "Nadya's parents are both dead. What male relative will speak for her at her wedding?"

"Her older cousin. If both sides agree, then we'll witness her betrothal ceremony, the *pliashka*," Misha replied.

Luca grinned. "I haven't been gone a decade, Misha. I know what a *pliashka* is."

The insistent clip of horses' hooves stopped Luca from continuing. He raised a forefinger to his lips and stood without making a sound. "Ssh. Someone's coming."

CHAPTER TWELVE

"Highwaymen," Misha came to his feet alongside Luca. "They're in the wrong place. There's nothing to rob here."

Before Luca could reply, a stocky, imposing man wearing a black cloak, ambled across the stream in the direction of the small group. The women on the barn door screamed and dashed for their tents. All the elders except for Misha fled.

Another hulking man, even larger, emerged from the forest, his movements measured and deliberate, his cold, flinty gaze pointed at Luca.

Luca's heart pounded in double time. He fingered the sheath of his dagger concealed in his tall, brown boot. "What do you want?" He kept his tone calm as he scanned the forest for more attackers.

"We were told there were Gypsies camping in this area," the stocky man said.

"Now that you've seen us, you can move on," Luca said.

He glanced toward the children on the hammock and nodded to one of the women. She grabbed the children and ushered them to the fringe of the camp.

"Where's this dog's collar?" the stocky man asked, jerking his chin towards the lean dog. He snorted. "You're all dogs. Where are all your collars?"

Luca stiffened. The air had turned predatory in a blink. The insults he'd heard so many times before, he was tired of them, tired of protecting his people, good people, from bad English men.

The stocky man sauntered closer to the campfire where Luca and Misha stood. "You're damaging the grass beneath the snow."

Luca swallowed and focused on holding his temper in rein. "Keep your distance," he gritted. Legs a foot apart, shoulders rigid, his stance shifted to one trained for fighting. If these men were waiting to see him or any of his tribesmen fall, they'd be sadly mistaken.

Luca glanced at the tents and the numerous pairs of black eyes peering from the openings.

Then his gaze locked on a set of ham like fists.

"Do you have anything of worth that you've stolen?" The other, bulky man regarded Misha. "Gold coins can aid us in keeping yer secret of encroaching on other people's land and owning dogs without collars."

"This is forest land and belongs to no one," Luca said before Misha could speak. "When the weather breaks, we'll leave peacefully."

The stocky man grabbed a branch from the ground and snapped it at Luca. "We can find you dirty Gypsies anywhere because of yer smell."

Luca reached for his knife. Nay. He didn't want to fight these men. He didn't want to carry the guilt, the knowledge that what he did was wrong. The bulky Englishman skulked closer, together a vibrating haze of hostile mouths and bloodless eyes.

Luca grasped the handle of his dagger. He had no choice,

because the tribe needed to be protected. "Don't do anything you'll be sorry for," Luca warned.

"The law wants to be rid of Gypsies littering our land, moving around so quick to hide your criminal activities."

"Leave us alone," Misha shouted.

The stocky man lunged at Misha. "Stay out of this, old man."

Misha surged forward and rammed into the stocky man's beefy chest. The man crumpled and a rickety tent collapsed beneath them both.

Without warning, the other, bulky man leapt forward and struck Luca in the groin, knocking Luca to his knees. Luca jerked in nauseating pain and let go of the dagger. Fury at his own foolishness for not being on guard pushed him to his feet. He risked a glance behind to be sure the tribe was safe. The saucer-eyed faces of the elders stared back at him.

The hulking man struck a heavy jab into Luca's chest. He threw Luca back to the ground, his heavy boot landing on Luca's leg.

"Worthless Gypsy," he tsked, eyeing Luca with brutal disinterest. "Where are all the men from your tribe? Are they cowards like you?"

Luca rolled to the side and willed himself to his feet. Every muscle on edge, he rubbed his split lips, wringing a silent rasp from his throat. There were two men. Both had attacked. If there were any more, he wouldn't be able to defend the tribe.

With an inhuman roar from the stocky man, a sharp-edged pair of steel boots lifted and smashed into Luca's right thigh. Luca's legs caved. Distorted shouts rumbled above him.

Bile hardened in his throat. He braced for the fiery stab of a jagged knife or the ball of a pistol shot into his ribs. He couldn't make sense of his mangled thoughts.

"My friend told you to leave." Through the cacophony of

English jeers and curses, Pulko's deep voice rose above the din with a sharpness that Luca had never heard before.

Slowly, Luca raised his head. Pulko stood solemn, aiming a pistol directly at the stocky Englishman. In unison, the two Englishmen raised their hands in surrender.

"Don't say a word," Pulko cautioned. "Just go."

The men didn't nod, didn't acknowledge that they'd heard Pulko. They scurried through the underbrush and into the forest. Soon the sound of horses' hooves clipped rapidly away.

Sprawled on the wet ground, Luca kept his eyes open, aware of the pain mushrooming in his skull. His leaden leg throbbed. Slush and dirt invaded his nostrils. A loud groan pierced the silence. His own damn, helpless voice. He glided his fingers down his cloak for the dagger in his boot, to be sure it hadn't been taken in the struggle.

Squeezing his eyes shut to control the pain, he staggered to his feet. He squinted through the tree limbs to focus on Pulko, but his vision wouldn't cooperate. Overhead, a murky stream of stars obscured the twilight.

"Where did you get the pistol?" he managed.

"I stole it," Pulko replied evenly.

Luca braced both hands on his knees. A penetrating jolt of agony shot up his leg, humbling him. Fog clouded his brain, but one message from the English screamed in his ears.

Be gone from England. Gypsies don't belong here.

CHAPTER THIRTEEN

*T*wo more weeks passed. Two more weeks of rain and dreariness and dread of being attacked again. Adding to the dread, Pulko mentioned that Marko had been spotted at the outskirts of Lady Blakwell's property.

Luca felt his muscles tense. Arms folded across his chest, he peered at the hills surrounding the camp. He waited a minute to speak, trying to best phrase his thoughts to Pulko and Fabiana, who stood nearby.

"I'm returning to Lady Blakwell's estate for a visit because I don't want her vulnerable and in danger from Marko," he said.

In truth, he couldn't stop himself from going back to see her.

"What about us?" Fabiana asked.

"Pulko can begin leading the tribe to Colchester when the weather breaks and I'll join you shortly."

Fabiana's thin eyebrows formed two distinct arcs. She opened her mouth, but Luca raised his hand to continue. "I cannot lead our tribe wisely when my senses are slowed by continuous pain. Lady Blakwell's maid had applied a special liniment made from a white powder that relieved the throbbing in my leg. I should've brought the liniment with me when I departed, but I didn't."

"A Roma's liniments are more powerful than any English."

Luca leaned toward Fabiana. "This particular liniment eased my discomfort. Since the English's recent attack, my leg aches worse than ever."

Pulko held out his arms to push Luca and his mother apart. "You're leaving because of what I told you about Marko being spotted near Lady Blakwell's estate."

"'Tis only a short visit," Luca said.

Fabiana fingered a cord of tinkling bells tied to her bodice. The inky pouches beneath her eyes swelled as her gaze narrowed. "Pulko's too young to be left alone and lead the tribe."

Pulko put his large hands on his hips. "I'm not too young."

Luca took in the muscles in Pulko's arms. Pulko seemed to grow stronger with each passing day.

Noncommittal, Luca accorded his dripping *bender* another glance. The hazel twigs holding up the roof looked in danger of caving. A film of green mold grew at an astounding rate up the side of the canvas.

He directed his gaze to Pulko. "When you depart, follow the cattle path along the coast and travel south towards Colchester where the weather is warmer. If you need me for any reason, you can find me at Lady Blakwell's."

Fabiana grabbed Luca's cloak. "Don't let your impulsive nature steer you on another disastrous course. Less than three sennights ago, you allowed hunger and desperation to cloud your judgment. The spirits were furious as a result, you could've lost your leg, and Nadya was also brutally beaten. Nevertheless, you tempt fate again for a woman. An English noblewoman."

She spit at the ground.

"'Tis perilous for Lady Blakwell to be alone," Luca said. "She's defenseless."

Luca and Fabiana scowled at each other, two stubborn Roma from different ages, quarreling beneath a soaked, torn canopy. "I'd appreciate a pair of Pulko's woolen hose, if you can spare them."

Fabiana retied her peacock blue scarf around her head and gave the ends an infuriated yank, then reached into her tent and slipped Luca the hose. "Be careful," she said.

"Aye. Thank you." He accepted the hose, scooped his pouch from the ground, and snatched his walking stick.

Luca walked to Besnik sitting near his tent. "Can I borrow my hawking gloves?" he asked.

"Going hawking, are ye? Coming round to the English gentry, although they nearly killed us?" The old man's frown went so deep Luca imagined he could fit a shilling in the wrinkles. With a humph, Besnik rubbed his gloved hands together, then wrenched off the gloves and threw them to Luca.

Luca pulled them on, flexing his fingers into the layers of black leather, brushing his thumb against the fine gathering of fringe on the cuff. He admired the painstakingly embroidered initials in gold thread. E.H. The initials certainly weren't his, nor anyone he knew. He shook his head. There was such extraordinary wealth in England, such extraordinary poverty.

"I'll take great care of E.H.'s gloves," Luca replied wryly, then swung toward the woods.

Oddly, the throbbing in his leg subsided with each measured step. Rather than declare his astonishing recovery to Fabiana and Pulko, Luca trudged past the campfires, past the tents, past the crude stable. He headed west, leaving behind his cherished tribesmen and an uncomfortable silence.

⁓

*T*wice, Luca considered abandoning his decision to visit Lady Blakwell's estate while leaving his tribe unguarded. He even feared his attraction to her might've blurred his common sense. But he couldn't stop himself from returning. He needed to see her, be with her, regardless of the fact that he could never live a foreign, English life.

Briefly, he closed his eyes and rubbed his forehead, weighing the pros and cons of his decision. He didn't consider himself a hero. He considered himself an ordinary man, trying to accomplish not-so-heroic feats. He felt split in two —trying to guard both her and his tribe.

Aye, she was brave and had more than her share of spirit and mettle, but hidden beyond the façade he detected vulnerability. She possessed neither the ability nor resources to fight off a vengeful Roma lord a second time. Save for Penham and Amelia, her houseful of servants proved eerily inept.

Perhaps Luca could ask Patience to join his tribe, and she could live there safely with him.

He blew out a breath and shook his head. Unfortunately, many in his tribe would wish harm upon her and wouldn't accept her. It was ridiculous to think they could ever share a future together, even if he did have English blood flowing in his veins. Besides, Amelia had told him about Patience's stepson's threatened murder charge. Her stepson would lay charges for sure, and the law would come after Patience.

And why, Luca wondered matter-of-factly, did she bring about this protective urge in him? After more than two decades of hating the English, he, a Romany clothed in rags, was off to an English estate to protect an Englishwoman in a silken black mourning dress while abandoning his tribe in the process.

The afternoon warmed. Lulled by the tap-tap-tap of a

steady rain, Luca managed to cover the distance to Lady Blakwell's estate in half the time he expected.

Perhaps she'd missed him when she wasn't occupied with her many responsibilities. Overseeing an estate was complicated, especially for a young widow. He'd never known a beautiful female who could juggle more than a few tasks without dissolving into tears. The dowager countess, a refined Englishwoman, accomplished her challenges with a calmness and devout faith belying her small stature.

He pictured her expression when he arrived at her doorstep. She'd surely rush to him.

The thought made him smile.

At the riverbank bordering her property, he paused to take in the vastness of the estate, the open, barren fields, the fences surrounding them, a wooden bench long abandoned. Etched into a limestone wall was the silhouette of a cross with heavenly creatures floating above with great white wings. His gaze rose from the arched entry to the large chimneys.

The house seemed different now. So welcoming.

He reached the kitchen herb garden a few minutes later and viewed Amelia through the window. She bustled in the kitchen with no other servants about. He rapped on the door and braced himself for the maid's receptive squeal of joy. She'd become an unanticipated friend and ally.

The door swung open. Wide-eyed, Amelia reeled. "Mr. Gypsy, what are you doing here?"

Unconsciously, he massaged his throbbing leg. He set his walking stick on the threshold and retied Pulko's hose around his knee. "'Tis a rumor that Marko's prowling about Ipswich and I won't leave Lady Blakwell vulnerable to danger."

And, he realized, he just hated not seeing her.

He glanced about the pantry and the kitchen beyond, inhaling the warm and welcoming smell of buttery biscuits.

Amelia clasped her hands together, a strained smile on her plump face. "Lady Blakwell isn't here. She's in town, meeting with a solicitor, giving him details about Lord Crispin's murder charge. The solicitor will then hire a barrister to represent her case before a judge. She should return with news of her meeting by later this evening."

"Lady Blakwell is innocent of murder," Luca said.

He thought of their previous conversation when Amelia had tended to him in the attic. Amelia had told him that Patience's evil stepson was coercing her cooperation in the matter of the estate with a threatened murder charge.

"Aye," Amelia said. "However, her stepson is tight with legal types and he'd be able to make the charges stick. In any event, she'll need funds to try and fight this case. Funds, unfortunately, that she doesn't have."

Again, Luca revisited the thought that if it was just a matter of being at the economic mercy of her stepson, Luca could ask her to join his tribe. However, his tribe wouldn't approve, and the law would surely be at her heels.

Despite that thought, his breath came easier as he swung his arms and entered the hallway. He'd see her later that evening, when she returned. Then they could discuss the matter further.

CHAPTER FOURTEEN

*L*uca headed to the attic to hide from the servants.

He'd assumed that Patience would be overjoyed to see him. And she was.

Except that she'd seemed preoccupied and quiet regarding her meeting with the solicitor, stating that the solicitor hadn't been encouraging that she'd win her case. She'd looked tired, and defeated, and Luca had encouraged her to retire early with promises that they'd talk in the morning.

Consequently, Luca had been unable to bring up the subject of her returning to his tribe with him, nor come up with another plan to protect her. And, he hadn't wanted to worry her regarding Marko so he'd said nothing except that he'd returned for her maid's liniment (partly true), and to ensure that Patience was safe.

He'd spent the remainder of the evening, hidden and out of sight, combing the outer fields of her estate. There'd been no signs of Marko nor his men.

Patience and he had both agreed that any moments together were risky and that Luca should stay hidden in the attic. Lord Crispin would charge Patience with scandalous, inappropriate behavior if he'd heard she'd harbored a Gypsy in her home, which could be used against her in his murder accusations.

And if all of this weren't bad enough, Luca's leg pained him worse than ever, although the pain didn't stop him from combing the woods one more time late that evening, searching for an absent Marko.

Instead, Luca met up with a *vurma* who'd told Luca that his tribe had quit their previous camp and had begun traveling along the cattle path en route to Colchester.

"A *vurma* is a Roma woman who keeps track of the Romany tribes and knows where they travel, because Roma have no addresses to speak of," Luca explained patiently to Amelia.

Although the hour was late, Amelia had returned to the attic to tend to him, rolling up his buckskin breeches and examining his wound. The linen cloths around his leg were tacky, the largest gash festering. With a worried frown, she'd admitted that her special liniment was proving ineffective and Luca needed a more powerful cure. Rather than the physician in town that everyone knew, she suggested a barber-surgeon several towns over who was a friend of hers and wouldn't divulge that Luca was hiding out in Lady Blakwell's attic.

This particular man cut hair and shaved beards. And dressed gashes, pried out teeth, and severed limbs from a man's body.

Luca swore he'd never allow a barber who also posed as a surgeon to come anywhere near his leg, or Luca would run the barber out of England, thus shortening the man's diverse trades.

The tension in the attic escalated. Amelia seemed to sense his aggravation and kept a respectable distance.

"I'd like to spend some time with Lady Blakwell before I depart tomorrow," he said.

Amelia assured him that Lady Blakwell would come to the attic to see him.

Luca waited, standing by the attic window and scrutinizing the surrounding fields, searching for any sign of Marko and his men.

He eyed the pallet and rubbed his sore leg. Perhaps he should sleep for a few hours.

~

*L*uca awoke with a start as Amelia clattered in.

"How are you this fine morning?" she asked cheerfully, disregarding the sullen clouds hovering beyond the attic window. Amelia carried a tray laden with roasted pork and a pot of coffee. Luca's stomach railed at the beastly smell of shriveled, overcooked meat.

"What time is it?" Luca stretched the kinks from his muscles on the ridiculously small pallet Patience had provided. His gaze didn't stay centered and he blinked, not knowing where to focus. Amelia's face smudged into two indistinct Amelias, with distorted red features and perpetually crooked knitted shawls.

He chafed his hands across his whiskered chin, feeling quick-tempered and lethargic. "Tell Lady Blakwell I'm returning to my tribe by noon," he said. "Did she visit me last night?"

"Aye, but you slept so soundly she didn't want to wake you." Amelia paused to take a breath. She set the tray beside Luca on a small oak table, knelt on the pallet, and touched his brow. "My word, you're feverish." She raised her eyes upward and whispered a silent prayer.

Then she threw off the assortment of heavy quilts he'd bundled around himself when he'd grown cold during his sleep. His green sash and orange scarf were next, leaving him clad in his wrinkled linen shirt and breeches.

Amelia ran the back of her palm across his cheeks and frowned. "Pulko came by earlier, riding a gray mare that has seen better days. He didn't want to disturb you as your sleep was fitful. He tethered the horse in the fields so as not to be seen by the servants and I provided him with provisions." Amelia smiled reassuringly. "He said he'd circle back within the sennight after the tribe makes camp."

"I'll return to the tribe before then." Luca shook off her hand and fairly growled. "Yesterday, I was unable to hike any farther than the boundary of the woods without tiring, yet Pulko came from near the coast and back in one day."

"He didn't walk as you did, he rode a horse and drove the horse hard. He's a very capable young man, as quick and sure-footed as you'll soon be again."

Luca shifted to ease the numbness. "My tribe needs me."

"Impatience hinders your recovery. I will pray. You will rest."

"I intend to repay you and Lady Blakwell tenfold for your kindnesses."

Amelia aimed a stern glare at him. "You can repay me foremost by confessing to Lady Blakwell what Pulko has been up to these past few sennights. Indeed, I cannot believe he talked me into being a part of such a shameful plan. Lady Blakwell doesn't mind sharing whatever food she has, but she'll be very unhappy when she discovers that Pulko has been stealing from her pantry with my permission."

Luca massaged his leg. "Pulko isn't stealing, merely borrowing, until I can provide adequately for my tribe when they reach the coast. I'll tell her myself what Pulko's been doing."

"She'd forgive you anything." Amelia hoisted to her feet and pulled up a stool. Using shears, she cut a heap of clean linen cloths and stacked them in a pile. "Draw your breeches to your knee." She covered the stool with her stout body and unbound the old cloths from Luca's leg.

Together, they eyeballed the ghastly sight of his inflamed wound.

Luca winced, the cloths weighty and wet as they slid down his leg.

Without an outward sign of emotion, Amelia said, "I need to call for the barber-surgeon or a doctor."

"Nay. No barber. No doctor."

"Awright, then," she demurred, holding up a vial of white powder. "We'll try my special liniment one more time."

"No liniment." He viewed the tray and shuddered. "No food, either."

"Drink the coffee. I ground a twinge of toadstool in the brew."

Luca leveled her with a baleful gaze. "Toadstool is poisonous."

"Toadstool will help you sleep."

"I slept enough. I'm leaving." He sipped the pungent, hot brew to appease her, until his throat refused to swallow another drop. His limbs felt weak. Perhaps he could rest a few more minutes.

"My lady will come to check you," Amelia said.

He thought he smelled panic in her voice.

~

*S*omewhere between the twilight of sleep and wakefulness, Luca felt heavy quilts tangling about his legs. He heard hurried footsteps on the attic stairwell, doors creaking and slamming, distraught whispers somewhere nearby. He cried out in frustration, trying to escape the nightmares of chasing something he could never reach, no matter how hard nor how fast he ran.

He raked a hand across his face and tried to force himself awake. "'Tis only a dream," he told himself. "Only a dream."

His breaths came short and shallow. His heart pumped too fast. In his native Romanes tongue he cried out, but no one heard him, because the louder he cried, the more silent his shouts became, an empty scream leaving him sick and weak.

Whenever he nodded off again, worse dreams, ever more terrifying, swelled his thoughts. Before his paralyzed eyes his leg withered to a small stump, like the end of a rotted cat's tail. Then his leg fell away, a never-ending freefall down a bottomless moat. He dove into the frigid, filthy water to find his leg, felt his chest burning to breathe, and dove deeper. He thought he saw the elders of his tribe at the murky bottom. At last he found them. He needed to save them. But his strokes were never strong, his breaths never powerful enough to reach them.

Other body parts fell off as well—a foot, a finger, an arm. He watched, helpless, sinking deeper, drowning alone in a watery grave. He couldn't swim, he shouted. He couldn't swim.

He awoke in a spasm of coughs and gasps, surrounded by Romany spirits of the night. The dreaded *martiya*.

Luca yanked the quilts from his leg and tried to focus, ensuring he was still whole.

What time was it?

Calm, he told himself. Stay calm.

When next he woke, the light glinting through the window was no longer the paleness of morn, nor the gray-white gleam of a winter afternoon. It was past twilight and a bright, full moon lit the sky.

He wasn't in his *bender*, his familiar tent. Nor was he

outside, for the air wasn't refreshing and cool. He breathed deeply and concentrated on the familiar quilts bundled around his legs, the row of fat candles flickering in their sconces on a table nearby, the thick wool rug added to his pallet atop the blankets.

Lady Blakwell's attic. He was in her attic, awaiting her return.

He visualized her sweet face and sank back. His dreams came easier.

~

Through a burn of sweat, Luca realized a woman knelt beside him. She'd been there a while, for he felt the warmth of her body. Her curly hair was loose about her shoulders, a fringe of refined red in the moonlight.

Patience.

He moaned, tried to grope for his walking stick to stand, tried to recall where he'd last set it down. His injured leg hampered his movements. He didn't want her to see him so powerless and feeble, like a pathetic cripple.

"Go away." He tried to speak, but his voice didn't comply.

Her hands grasped his shoulders and eased him back down to his pallet.

So tender. So kind. So compassionate.

"Save your strength," she whispered.

He attempted a protest but his mouth was dry and he was too tired to object. He kept his eyes half-closed and heeded the tears pooling at the corners of her eyes and streaking past her cruel scar.

"*Kamadiyo*," he whispered, struggling to smile. "You're crying."

I don't have the strength to race from the room to avoid your tears.

She sniffed and dabbed at her eyes with her fingers. "These aren't tears."

"Don't lie. I'm not dead yet."

She averted her face and sobbed, quietly. "You'll not die. Promise me."

"I never make a promise I cannot keep."

"Promise."

"For you, *kamadiyo*, I will try," he whispered.

She bent and dabbed a moist linen cloth to his wound. His back arched with the pain of it. She tried to be gentle, he knew she tried. He clenched his jaw, an effort not to moan as agony roared through him.

Her hands shook as she wrapped a clean cloth around his leg. "Amelia will come to the attic with her gingerroot brew. The herb cures most afflictions."

"The herb will not cure a corrupted leg." Luca tried to breathe deeply, great heaves to absorb the purity of Patience's air into his lungs. "Tell Amelia to send for Pulko. I want a report on the tribe's journey and need to know they're safe." Luca's head fell back on the pallet. The throbbing of the gash was incessant and rhythmic and weakened his heartbeat. Poison filled his insides with venom. He felt it, saw the poison blighting each tiny pore of his skin.

The early morning hours elapsed in vague silhouettes and murky shadows.

Sometimes he felt nothing, a freedom from his body. He was a spongy cork, light, free, bobbing in the air, watching himself from the ceiling. He hovered in a place that protected him from more pain than his body could handle.

Patience sang, her melodious voice easing him. He recognized bits of Latin although he'd never set foot in a church. Endless Kyries and Agnus Deis, sacred hymns of prayers.

She talked when she wasn't singing, clear and reassuring words, and he'd forsake this safe dreamlike state for the reality of her fingertips squeezing his hands, the warmth of her comforting breath on his cheeks.

She was an illusion, a sparkle of decency with a heart of grace. Surely she wasn't real, for there was little good in the harsh life he knew. But he sought her touch, her hymns and her prayers, for her cool fingers revived his fevered body and flawed soul.

He must've dozed, for Patience shook him awake.

"Mr. Boldor, Amelia added more toadstool to a fresh cup of tea to lessen your fever."

He tried to surface from his dreams, to become a part of Patience's world. "I cannot swallow," he protested. He forced himself to open his eyes. "Amelia is trying to kill me with toadstool."

Patience leaned over and held a dainty blue teacup steady. She smiled, the smile that told him to fight for his life.

He slept a while, awakening once more to the cup urged to his lips. Patience was agreeably close, her lavender fragrance filling the stench of the oppressive air. He never realized how much he liked lavender. Purple fields of lavender, rows and rows of sweetness. This was his life, a life full of unpredictable turns and purple lavender and dainty blue teacups.

She lightly kissed the bridge of his nose where it had once been broken and held out that damn, dainty teacup. "Drink."

"I don't like coffee with sugar in it," he said.

"Good, because this is tea. It will give you strength."

She offered falsehoods, her, a Christian woman. He'd never regain his strength, never again be physically able, because there was no remedy powerful enough to stop the venom that would kill him in a matter of hours. He felt the decay spreading through his body, breaking it down, bit by wretched bit. First rotting his useless leg, then his arms, then flowing through his blood until his heart stopped beating.

"You're doing splendidly." Patience brought the cup to his lips again.

His teeth chattered, making a light, sharp noise on the porcelain cup. He bit down on his dry mouth, licking the metallic taste of blood mixed with the potency of toadstool and tea with milk and sugar. His lips felt like charred pieces of bread scorched by a never-ending flame.

She dabbed a cool cloth to his forehead, whispering words of a prayer.

His head pitched back. Shadows dueled with awareness, darkness with light.

~

Sunlight poured through the attic window when Luca next opened his eyes. Patience knelt on the floor near him. "Mr. Boldor," she said. "Penham snuck your friend, Pulko, here."

Luca licked his cracked lips and swallowed. "How did you find Pulko?"

"Amelia told me about a *vurma*," Patience teased. "We're learning your language. Aren't you proud of us?"

"Infinitely proud." Luca blinked to awareness and twisted up too fast from the depths of a comforting dream, although he couldn't remember the details. Tiny flares erupted behind his eyelids. The attic whirled, his stomach rolled. He grabbed for Patience's fingers to steady himself.

Pulko gaped down at Luca. His cheeks were ruddy with vigor, his sable eyes awash in sadness and concern.

With Patience's assistance, Luca sat up. "How's the tribe?" he asked.

"Everyone's well. We made camp near the sea." Pulko pushed aside his frayed cloak, which fluttered strangely. With a triumphant flourish, he raised a scratching and clacking black hen. Skinny claws hung from Pulko's fingers, a pointed bill pecked at his wrists, and black wings flapped furiously.

"I brought you this hen," Pulko said.

"So I see," Luca said skeptically.

"My mother said that a black hen will help you get well."

"Did your mother want the hen to peck a sick man to death?"

"Amelia will boil the hen and split it in two. All you have to do is eat it."

"Black hens cost far too much coin."

Pulko shrugged and held the flapping hen high. "I stole the hen so I used no coin. The *gadje* farmer didn't need the hen. He had two."

Luca glanced at Patience. He expected her eyebrows to converge, her frown accusatory for Pulko's crime of stealing. Instead, she pointed to a tray holding three jugs of water. "After you eat the hen, Fabiana wants you to drink some water from the stream."

"And here's some wood." Amelia stepped forward from the eaves of the attic with several hazelnut branches. "We must throw these into the fireplace to keep you warm. Pulko and Penham will assist us in moving you back to your former bedchamber, and we shall make fine use of the fireplace."

Luca's bones trembled with the effort, but he agreed, feeling the first measure of hope in days. He couldn't help but grin, watching a squawking, pecking hen and dry hazelnut branches waggling in his direction.

Patience held him upright, her small fingers clamped around his forearm.

"Do you believe in Romany ways for healing sickness?" he asked.

She gave him a cheeky perusal. "I have the greatest confidence in anything Gypsy. This will ease your mind, and we'll add prayers to God."

"I made a poultice of butter and onions for your leg," Amelia added. "And I'll cleanse your wound mornings and evenings with a salve made from vinegar, although it may burn a bit. Between your Gypsy remedies and God's mercy, I predict you'll spring from your bedchamber within a fortnight."

"And I'll be good enough to eat," Luca said.

With effort, Pulko and Penham steadied Luca on the pallet and carried him down the attic stairwell to the guest bedchamber one floor below. Then, Pulko assured that he'd slip quickly from the house to return to the tribe.

Slats of a mid-winter sun pushed through the window and brightened the room. Luca's eyes feasted on the sight of the familiar bedchamber and the heartening blaze in the fireplace.

Penham assisted Luca with his private needs and helped him bathe. Once Luca was settled on the bed, Patience set a tray before him, a steaming trencher of boiled hen enhanced by a touch of rosemary. She fed him several morsels of cooked hen, giving him sips of water from the jugs after each swallow.

He lifted his head like a broken bird. Chewing, swallowing, helpless. After interminable bites, the bedchamber whirled, and Luca sank wearily onto the feather mattress.

"I'll eat more in a while," he assured, noting the protest poised on Patience's lips. He refused her cup of water. He intended to doze.

A few minutes later, he heard Amelia and Patience speaking by the fireplace.

"He constantly fears he'll lose his strength," Patience said.

"Between the wormwood and gingerroot I stirred into his water, he'll sleep for several hours," Amelia said, then sighed. "Unfortunately, in addition to the healing effects of the potions, there may be other difficulties."

Patience stopped, dried hazelnut branch in hand. "What sort of difficulties?"

"He may forget what occurred last evening. His nightmares, his screams of pain. The body has ways to blot out suffering." Amelia slanted a kindly glimpse in Luca's direction. "His wits may be slowed until he makes a full recovery."

"I'm inclined to favor his health over any temporary lack of wit," Patience said.

"On the other hand, he's strong. Perhaps he'll rally with no ill effects."

"He's endured enough pain for twenty men. He came back to be sure that I was safe and ended up suffering because of his tiring journey." Patience pitched the last of the hazelnut branches into the fireplace. She wiped her hands along her black frock and retied the knot of her paisley shawl. "I'll see to dinner preparations, then return to him for the evening."

"I'll come downstairs shortly. One more dose of water and he'll sleep through the night like a newborn babe," Amelia said.

Patience clicked the bedchamber door shut, her footsteps scurrying down the stairwell.

Amelia tweaked a piece of gingerroot and wormwood from the plants she'd placed by Luca's bedside and crushed the herbs into the water. She held the cup up to the late afternoon sunlight streaming from the window and stirred a second time.

She stepped on the stool, and leaned over. "How's my favorite Gypsy patient?" She blinded him with a bright, toothy grin and swished the water. "Feeling better?"

He fixed her with a slow-burning glower so threatening that she dropped the cup and spilled the water onto the wooden floor. She flew from the stool and grabbed some linen cloths by the bed. When her gaze finally bounced back to his, he snapped, "I feel in excellent health. However, I'll never be able to tolerate the sight of another black hen."

"Aye," she agreed. "But water's just the thing for—"

He pushed to a sitting position on the bed. "If you're waiting for me to drink another drop of your tainted water, then pull up a cushioned stool and fetch a great deal of knitting, for you'll be waiting a long, long time."

CHAPTER FIFTEEN

A fortnight had passed since Luca's feverish night in the attic. He'd made a full recovery thanks to a Romany cure of hazelnut branches and a black hen.

He smiled. Honesty prompted him to shake his head. His recovery was because of Patience's prayers and ministrations.

He'd wanted to be up and gone at least a sennight before now, because his tribe needed him. However, Amelia and Patience had disagreed, asserting that Pulko was handling the day to day activities of the tribe, and that Luca would hinder his recuperation by doing too much, too soon, and consequently suffer a relapse.

Worn out from a morning of digging holes and repairing fences, Luca leaned on his shovel and stared at the grounds of Patience's estate. He'd worked in a field at the edge of her property to ensure that none of the servants could see him.

All his bones ached, and he wiped a dirty hand to push the hair from his forehead. He'd climbed to the top of the knoll, which gave him an impressive view while he searched for an absent Marko. The hills were open, the midday sun melting the snow that earlier powdered the lanes.

The hedgerows, a plush green, threaded through the moorland and separated the pastures. White sheep and black cattle grazed the highlands, a sleepy halcyon scene of salt and pepper.

He took in a bracing whiff of fresh air, thin and clear. A fine day, and uncommonly pleasant. He drove the shovel into the ground and turned up his breeches. Sweat poured from his temples and he wiped his brows. A good sweat, from hard work and warm sunshine. He cast off his cloak and rolled up the sleeves of his linen shirt.

"Mr. Boldor!" Patience shouted, effectively replacing his thoughts of her with her actual self. Her body seemed, fuller, rounder, which meant that she was healthy. With one hand lifting the hem of her berry frock, she emerged from a clearing of willow trees at the bottom of the knoll. She waved and made her way around a rusty pond, stepping along the wet ground. "No more digging. You're not one of the servants."

Luca rubbed his bottom lip and briefly closed his eyes.

He wasn't a servant. He was a dirty Gypsy. Hated by most, looked down on by all.

He opened his mouth to correct her, but thought better of it. No need to begin their conversation with a disagreement, for she'd surely become indignant and gush about him being a man of honor, of virtue. A *bulibasha*. A lord of his tribe.

His tribe, he thought grimly. His care for their welfare was most delinquent. He wasn't an honorable, virtuous man. He was a neglectful lord, thinking naught of others, only of himself.

He had to get back to them.

He wiped his dirt-stained hands on his breeches. In truth, he wasn't ready to leave Patience. He had to be near her, near her convictions, near her truth.

Patience trudged through the mud, her velvet frock raised enough to expose the tips of her black boots beneath pantaloons. Her fur-trimmed pelisse was dark green, swinging open as she walked, a velvet belt tied above her waist. Her hair was completely hidden by a tight-fitting linen mob cap, leaving her freckled face exposed. Her cheeks were pale beneath the flush of exertion.

"Are you mad?" she asked as she reached him. "You're still weak. Amelia said you bathed this morn and you might catch a chill if you stay outdoors." She wiped at the smudges of dirt on his forehead with her gloved fingertips.

He took her gloved hands in his. "I'm hardly working and I'm hardly weak."

"You've been digging in these fields since early morn. This is the first day Amelia pronounced you healthy enough to venture outdoors, but she meant for you to go for a walk, not dig a ditch."

"According to Amelia, I'm better. According to me, I was better a sennight ago. I spent my days peering out the bedchamber window at these forgotten fields."

He looked in the direction of the fields and grimaced.

Patience followed his gaze. "The fields are neglected. With no dower, I can hardly pay the servants' wages. Only Lord Crispin benefits from any Blakwell fortune."

She'd misunderstood Luca's grimace, thinking he didn't approve of the sorry state of her fields, although he was grateful for the change in subject.

Luca stroked the knuckles of her hands. His gaze rested on the dark circles beneath her eyes, the paleness of her complexion. "You look tired of late."

"I suffer nausea whenever I smell vinegar."

"Amelia rinsed my gash with vinegar over a sennight ago."

"The tart smell lingers along with bad memories."

"Not bad memories of me, I hope."

Her eyebrows knit into a frown. "Nay. I breathe my late husband's medicine and the vinegar forces me to remember your suffering."

She was extraordinary, always worrying about him. She was the fragile English rose blooming in a spring garden, fresh and fragrant, lavender, mixed with the floral breeze of wildflowers.

He thought about kissing her, forsaking all boundaries of propriety. He tamped down his thoughts by focusing on his surroundings—the chirping of a nightjar, the gentle wind on his face, the drone of the first honeybees of the season.

He took in a long breath until his heartbeat slowed.

A knowing smile wreathed her face. "Obviously, you've recovered."

'Twas the Romany in him, he rationalized, his instinctual urge to kiss her outdoors under a vivid blue sky. But Patience was exquisite and delicate. She deserved to be courted wearing silk and satin, in a room decorated in fine lace and velvet.

He shifted. The longer he stayed in the *gadje's* world, the more accustomed he became to their comforts. He risked forgetting his own Romany world, and all that the tribe had done for him.

He met her doe-eyed gaze and smiled. He'd fought his way through life as a man in pursuit of goodness and fairness. He'd never come across either, but here they stood, wrapped in a cloth of English respectability, while his Romany obligations pulled him away.

Amelia called from beyond the hill. She and Penham sprang from a small wagon carrying several wicker baskets and a table.

Patience grinned. "If you're up to it, I planned a picnic, far away from the prying eyes of the housemaids."

"What's a picnic?" Luca asked.

"'Tis enjoying food outdoors, " she said, "especially on a lovely day like this."

"I've eaten outdoors all my life and the Rom never called roasted rabbits on a spit a picnic."

She chuckled, childlike in her enthusiasm, as Amelia approached and assisted her with the baskets. "We'll not be eating roasted rabbit. I prefer tea with cream and rolls with butter."

Luca peeked inside the basket, grabbed a braised chicken leg, and grinned apologetically at Patience.

Amelia set the makeshift table with plates and silverware. "There's cold roast beef and plum pudding too."

"And a tin of biscuits," Penham added.

An hour later, the midday sun had turned the sky into a painting, an array of blue and pink punctuated with white clouds. Luca sat on the ground with his back against an oak tree.

"I like picnics," he said.

Patience stared at the open sky. "I'm glad."

"What's so interesting?"

"I look up and try to take it all in. The vastness of creation humbles me."

Luca stared upward, then back at the leftover chicken legs packed in the wicker baskets. "Your English picnic is an excellent idea. Next time I'll tell Amelia to add Rom food, perhaps a roasted hedgehog."

Next time, the assurance of another time, of a promise that he'd share another picnic with Patience in a setting as perfect as this one.

She laughed. "A roasted hedgehog doesn't sound very appetizing."

"You can fry it in butter, but roasting is better."

Patience glanced in the direction of the wagon and

nodded at Amelia. "We should return to the dower house before it gets any later."

He helped the servants dismantle the table. At the sight of Patience's raised eyebrows, he grinned teasingly. "Did you think that I wasn't able to clean up after myself? Roma men are known for their neatness."

They weren't and they both knew it, and they both laughed.

With a curtsey and a bow, Amelia and Penham finished wrapping the food, carried it back to the wagon, and departed.

"Where's your walking stick?" Patience asked as she and Luca made their way back toward the dower house.

"'Tis burning in the guest bedchamber fireplace," he said sharply.

"Suppose you stumble and fall? I'll make you another one."

"I walk well on my own two legs and don't need a third."

"Because you think that relying on others makes you less of a man?"

"Because I'm a legend." He placed his hand in hers as he guided her down the slippery knoll and along the broken flag-stone paths. So easy they strolled together, talked together, joked together.

He'd hated the English all his life, but this woman was good-natured and intelligent, not a pampered, helpless crea-ture. She was loving, compassionate, and giving. Someone who took joy in every aspect of life, whether she was bent over her ledgers which she'd brought to the attic, although the ledgers never seemed to add up correctly, or sitting by the paned glass attic window, her dog snuggled in her lap.

They slid onto a slushy trail while she pointed to the sodden meadows and wide expanses of land. "Soon the wildflowers will take over these fields in all manner of delightful shades."

She seemed blissfully unaware of his thoughts as she continued to name every species of plant to ever grace England's shores, including many he had no interest in ever learning.

"Spear and thistle, thyme and chamomile," she was saying, "in addition to asters and violets and goldenrod." She pointed to a row of hawthorn hedges. "The walled garden beyond is crumbled, but once was filled with butterflies."

"And newts." Luca directed his gaze downward.

"Such disagreeable creatures. They resemble lizards." She lifted her feet, avoiding a gray newt darting past her feet, two distinct rust-colored blotches highlighted its jutting ribs. The brush of its long tail slid along the hem of her frock. She shrieked and held tightly to his arm.

"I dreamt of newts when I was ill," Luca said. "They're extraordinary creatures with an astounding ability to grow new limbs, new jaws, and even new eyes. A newt wouldn't have to endure the nightmare of losing a limb."

Patience squeezed his forearm in a fierce, shielding gesture. A fortnight ago, when he was ill, she'd held his hands in the same way. And when he'd first collapsed at her doorway, broken and discouraged, she'd knelt beside him. His woman of prayer, guarding him from all harm.

"Don't speak of nightmares for they're not real." Her shoulders straightened, as if every fiber of her was being prepared for an imaginary battle. "If you'd lost your leg—"

"I wouldn't be a man," he said.

"No limb, nor lack of a limb, defines you as a man, nor a burden."

He glanced at her, with her jaw set firmly, her gaze focused on the muddy trail ahead.

"A Roma man without the ability to run and hunt is no man at all."

She scoffed. "You spout foolish male arrogance."

As they neared the outskirts of the property, the laundry maids boiled clothes and hung them to dry.

Luca paused, pulling Patience behind a row of trees so that the laundry maids wouldn't see him. "I admit my male arrogance may be overbearing sometimes," he said.

She leaned into him, her body light and weightless. "Sometimes?"

The afternoon faded into streaks of orange as the sun lowered, wrapped in a scarf of amber. A squirrel jumped madly from branch to branch, rustling the trees while foraging for nuts. A tree swallow twittered, diving for insects. A songbird courted his female with a warbling mating call.

Feeling more lighthearted as the minutes slipped by, Luca laughed aloud. Patience stood on her toes and tipped her head back to peer at him.

"You're happy?" she asked.

"For the first time in a long while."

Her mouth curved into a smile. "As am I."

He couldn't help his grin because a lifetime's worth of affection lurked in her answer. And he was England's biggest fool for being attracted to a woman he had no right knowing, much less falling for. *Romni*. The thought came unannounced. His woman.

"My beautiful lady." Lightly, he touched the infinitesimal dimple peeking from the corner of her mouth. He'd ask her tonight to join him and travel back with him to his tribe. Damn the consequences.

Through an orchard of apple and pear trees, they walked the last few steps to the house's side entrance.

Their walk was interrupted by Pulko. His clothes were

rumpled beneath his muscled, strained forearms. He wiped at his over bright eyes, his gaze darting to Patience, then Luca.

"Luca, my mother is ill," Pulko said. "She...she wants to see you."

Luca felt his heartbeat race. Although they'd often quarreled, Fabiana had raised Luca since childhood. She'd been good to him, cared for him. He wouldn't refuse her request.

"Anything serious? Fabiana is never ill."

Pulko shook his head. "Nay, but she said 'tis time for you to return to the tribe. She told me to tell you that I can't hunt and fish and do everything on my own."

"We'll leave together at first light. Make camp and hide in the fields." Luca ran a jerky hand through his hair, then turned to Patience. "Fabiana is Pulko's mother, and the woman who raised me. I must leave. But before I do, I need to discuss something with you first."

CHAPTER SIXTEEN

*P*atience and Luca ate dinner together in the attic in silence. Amidst piercing thunderclaps and a ceaseless downpour, she swirled brown gravy around a crispy lamb cutlet, ate two spoonfuls of pea soup, and declined the sweet vanilla pudding topped with strawberries and meringue.

When dinner was cleared, Amelia and Penham retired for the evening.

"At last we're alone. No Amelia and no Penham," Luca said.

"Amelia is never far away," Patience replied.

Before she had the chance to cross the length of the attic, Luca had latched the attic door. Patience sat on a worn bench near the window, her fingers working rapidly on a piece of needlework. She closed her eyes, hearing his slight limp and the boyish urgency in his stride. She smiled at the outright stubbornness he'd exhibited in refusing to rely on a walking stick.

He was the most overwhelmingly handsome man she'd ever known, with his swarthy good looks, the ever-present ruby ring glimmering from his forefinger, his worn linen shirt billowing from his broad shoulders. Most important, he was healthy. With him, she felt out of harm's way and...cared for. He'd never told her as much, at least not in elaborate words. Surely his actions of ensuring her safety, his interest in her, spoke of emotions deeper than a passing fancy.

She gazed through the window's paned glass. His reflection behind her was a tall outline of rough edges and strapping shadows.

His fingers wrapped around her shoulders. "What are you thinking, *kamadiyo*?"

"I'm thinking of you," she replied honestly. "And that you'll be leaving again."

"I'll visit you when I can to be sure that you're safe."

She set down her needlework, stood, then placed her hands on his. Together, they stared into the darkened countryside lit by a full moon and the river beyond. She inhaled his nearness, the mysterious scent of moss caverns and oak forest floors.

"Ours is indeed an unusual...friendship," she said.

Her throat ached, wanting to replace friendship with courtship.

"*Kamadiyo*, you're beautiful," Luca said. "And I care about you more than you realize."

Now where had that come from? Nevertheless, the words sent a trembling up her spine. Aye, she cared for him, too, this man who couldn't be more wrong for her. Or more right.

Luca curved her round to face him. Merely inches separated them—but in reality there was a rift of diversity—two different social classes and lifetimes apart. Reality forced her to realize that it would take more than murmured Gypsy endearments to meld the gap.

"Pulko was agreeable about leaving at first light," Luca said.

"I hope he's comfortable sleeping in the fields."

Luca gazed out the window and said absently, "Aye, the fields are perfect."

Patience glanced at him. She enjoyed looking at him when he gazed elsewhere, for it gave her time to study him at leisure. She admired the expanse of his shoulders and his remarkably firm jaw. He gave her a sidelong glance and smiled. Of course, he knew she watched him. His black eyes were warm, a burning of charcoal in their depths.

"Do you need to sit?" she asked.

"Only if you're with me." He touched the knee of his breeches. "And if you fear for my health, my leg has never been better." Completely contradicting his assurance, sweat gathered above his lips.

Patience calculated the pain he must be experiencing multiplied by the hours he'd spent working in the fields. "'Tis time for you to rest before your journey on the morrow." She felt her chin tremble at the thought that he'd be leaving in a few hours.

His eyes lightened with amusement. "How much did you miss me last time I was gone and tending to my tribe?"

She gave her best attempt at a nonchalant smile and didn't answer.

Miss him? She dreamt of him. All the while thinking she meant nothing to him, convincing herself it mattered naught when he'd abruptly left her that night in the attic.

She rubbed the back of her neck. Weary from the strain of the past two fortnights when he'd been so ill, she gave up trying to analyze this mystifying man. Or his motives. Or her response to him.

He touched his lips to hers and whispered strange Gypsy words she didn't understand. She only understood that the realization of his departure brought an unforeseen twist to her heart.

He often compared her wealth and privilege to his hungry,

destitute tribe, but the wealthy were just as starving for love as the poor. She swallowed to dispel any silly notions of a future with him, any false expectations or fanciful daydreams. With a sigh, she drew back from him and stared down at her empty hands.

$\sim$

*L*uca noted Patience's stooped posture. Her eyes were lowered, her velvety eyelashes sweeping along her cheeks.

"When I'm in the English world, I feel like a knave who'll be charged with stealing something valuable," he said. "'Tis why I wanted to ask you...something."

Her posture straightened and she nodded, slowly. "What is it?"

He cleared his throat. "Would you...could you...travel back to my tribe with me when I leave in the morning? That way I know you'll be safe. You can stay as long as you'd like. I don't have money to offer, but I'll take good care of you."

He watched her hesitate, a wistful look in her gaze, before shaking her head. "I can't. You know I can't. My responsibilities are too great, and I must face my stepson's murder charge and fight back. I know that Amelia has discussed this issue with you."

"Would you come with me, were it not for his murder charge?" he asked softly.

The silence ticked by. He held his breath, waiting for a reply.

She focused on a point beyond him. "Perhaps."

His gaze found hers and she averted her eyes, as if she'd said too much. As if he'd seen more vulnerability than she'd wanted him to see. And he had. For he saw her fear, raw and exposed, on her face, in her voice, in the slight drop of her shoulders. The fear of rejection, and the shy admission of believing that she could trust him enough to be with him.

Her small hands fluttered about like two small birds, fumbling with her sleeves, smoothing her gown. The heady scent of her lavender soap on her skin was like a drug, a craving for all things Patience. He wanted to placate her with tender affirmations, but he'd never been one for elaborate words.

"You saved my life. In my haunted dreams, you were my hope," he said.

"You always make me feel protected and—"

Loved. His chest tightened. She hadn't said the last word, but he knew she was about to. He couldn't answer, nor fill in her sentence, because he'd never said the word to anyone.

He checked her fluttering hands. "Ssh," he whispered, which was all he could offer.

He prayed to God to help him, and wondered if God heard him, for no answer came.

He knew enough about women, this kind of woman, to know she'd never feel the same about him if he left and decided that he wouldn't return. And there was nothing for it, nothing he could do to stop the sadness, the realization that they could never be together.

He couldn't stay. He didn't belong here among the hated English. They'd been cruel, and unforgiving, and would never accept him.

A rousing white noise roared in his ears as he kissed her forehead. Perhaps they could live this way, die this way, hidden in their own, private attic without the interference of the outside world. The desperate thought passed through his mind. And then his mind stopped thinking when he gazed down at her beautiful face and the aching affection in her eyes.

Gently, he kissed her again. "My precious *wuzho*," he said. "Pure and untainted."

He held her, knowing he should let her go. He brushed an untamed, auburn curl from her cheek. The moonlight shining through the window transformed her creamy features to a burnished glow. How could he leave her? How could he stay? How could he abandon his tribe and lead an English life?

Patience stirred in his arms. She fulfilled him in a way no woman ever had. With her, he felt humored, his restiveness calmed, his spirit comforted.

Shyly, she smiled. "I want to show you something before you go." She whirled to her sewing basket and retrieved a sheet of paper beneath the colorful threads. She beamed as an excited child, her face lit by a maze of candlelight. "I have a gift for you."

His throat felt pinched and he swallowed. "I've never received a gift from anyone."

Patience gestured to the chair, pulled a stool next to him, and handed him the paper. Her earlier smile melted away and she peered at him beneath light, silky lashes. "Grant me the favor of accepting my gift and say thank you." She adopted the same low, persuasive tone he'd used in the attic two fort-nights earlier.

He unraveled the paper. In a simple drawing with black pen, she'd sketched him, remaining remarkably faithful to his features. He sat astride a lion with a thick mane and powerful haunches.

Luca held the sketch up to the candlelight. "You took great pains to keep the lines straight."

"At first I sketched you on a horse but the animal wasn't grand enough. I think of you as Richard the Lionheart."

"The pious English king?"

"Aye, although he spent little time in England. King

Richard composed poetry and was an adventurous man with a sense of honor."

"I never sat on a lion, nor composed poetry."

"You have a sense of honor like King Richard, and you're a noteworthy hunter."

"Did you save *my* sketch?" he prompted.

"Of course. I kept the two sketches together where I could look at them while I went about my day." She returned to her sewing basket and retrieved his sketch, tied carefully in a blue silk ribbon. "I've stared at it so often that the ink is starting to wear away."

A rustling outside the doorway made him pause. He set both sketches on a side table. "You should ask Amelia to prepare your bedchamber so that you can retire. Otherwise, I'm certain her ears shall burn off from eavesdropping."

"I'm not eavesdropping," Amelia's voice came from the other side of the attic door.

CHAPTER SEVENTEEN

*E*arly morning splashed into Patience's bedchamber and flooded her eyelids. Her mind was languid. Hazily conscious, she scrubbed her half-closed eyes with her fists and peered around her bedchamber.

Luca stood by the window, fully dressed in his linen shirt, breeches, and green sash. His overcoat was slung over his shoulders. Tied at the knee, the worn breeches exposed his well-muscled legs. His injured leg sported a thick linen bandage that looked as if it was recently cleaned and re-bandaged. His arms were crossed over his chest, his eyes focused on the fields.

She sat up in bed and yanked the comforter to her chin. "'Tis most improper to be in my bedchamber. A servant might see you. And how did you get in?"

Keeping his gaze toward the window, he said, "I wanted to ask you, one last time, if you'd come with me and live in my tribe."

She tucked the bed coverings securely around her and tried to reveal no emotion on her face.

The window was ajar and the sounds of servants shouting

to break the ice on the well were answered by the bark of a familiar dog. The pleasant, refreshing breeze through the window hinted of spring. Soon, the estate would come alive in brilliant color. Not everything passed away. Life was a never-ending cycle of promise and bright prospects. The thought comforted her.

He turned, his dark gaze intent and probing. No apologies for sneaking into her bedchamber and watching her sleep. Only the same question, which she'd answered the previous evening.

She wanted to avoid his question, for last evening she'd almost asked him, begged him, to do the same for her. *Please abandon your tribe, your people, your way of life. We'll find a way to fight Crispin.* Dear God, please understand. The more she was with Luca, the more she was beginning to realize that she needed him more than they did.

The previous evening in the attic, she'd been relieved that they'd been diverted, for if Patience had divulged her fears, of humiliation, and loneliness, and sadness, then the walls she'd erected to protect herself would indeed come tumbling down as the walls of Jericho, and Luca might feel obligated to give her more than he was able. She couldn't be another duty for him.

She drew a shaky breath. "You said you may visit again?" she hedged.

"Aye."

Then why couldn't he meet her eyes?

He shook his head, a denial, and seemed to struggle to find the right words. "Although I could never make a permanent home here."

Across the distance of the bedchamber, his words tolled matter-of-factly, like the harsh peal of a funeral clapper.

Her throat clogged with tears. "I never expected you to give up your obligations for me."

"My ties are to my people. I must travel where they travel because I owe them everything. They accepted me when I was alone and abandoned."

"Why this endless journey having no beginning or end?" She tried to mask the guarded hope in her voice. "Where is your home? What are you seeking?"

He strode to the bed and pressed a kiss on her cheek. He spread out his hands and surveyed her bedchamber. "This life, your English life with its endless rules, is the dreaded life of a *gadje*."

She tore her gaze from his. Wrapping the bedcovers around her muslin nightdress, she refused his hand of assistance and slipped from the bed. He turned and walked to the fireplace while she pitched her wrinkled berry frock over her head. When she was finished dressing, she walked to him. "There's no need to explain." She caught herself from saying more, knowing she'd sound clinging, besotted, like that adolescent girl who'd sought love so desperately that she'd begged her smooth-talking cousin to hold her after he'd hurt her.

Patience pushed back her shoulders, mentally encouraging herself. She was a dowager countess, for heaven sakes. She kept herself vigilantly composed, hands folded together at her waist, hardly moving.

"I know you were married once. I'm assuming you'll not be interested in any other man in my absence," he said.

She blinked. "What gives you the impudence to think you can control me when you offer nothing? Only the assurance of your absence."

"I said I'll visit whenever I'm able."

She rubbed her fingers along the neckline of her frock. "You spout an arrogant demand followed by a poor promise."

Under the stream of brash sunlight filtering through the window, Patience put a hand against the wall. She'd felt sick to her stomach since she'd awoken. She leaned her forehead on her hand.

"Go and live wherever you please," she said, with bracing sarcasm.

He grabbed her cold hands. "Suppose I want to stay right here but know that I can't because of my duty to my tribe?"

His voice was low and adamant, causing flashbacks of their hours together. His quiet whispers in his foreign tongue would forever resound in her mind. Attached to all those memories was the fact that she wanted him standing beside her in order to be complete. And she wanted him to feel the same.

Luca nodded slightly. As always, he read her thoughts. He brushed the hair from her face and brought her nearer. This was mad. They'd just quarreled.

Her fingers twined through his silky-smooth hair while his lips kissed her forehead.

Still, she felt a sense of dread. She ascribed the feeling to weariness. A weariness she'd suffered for many weeks.

"You heard Pulko. His mother said the tribe's lack of food necessitates my hunting skills as he can't do everything alone."

"Pulko can hunt. Pulko can guide."

"Not alone. And Pulko's young, only fifteen years old."

Her vision blurred. Her pulse rang disturbing screams of caution.

"What if something disastrous happens here while you're away?" she asked.

"From my exhaustive searches across your land, I'm assuming Marko gave up his need for vengeance and has gone back to his tribe in the south of England. I've seen no signs of him nor his men. If you need me, send Penham and I'll immediately return. He'll find the *vurma* on the cattle path along the sea and she can direct him to my tribe's camp." Luca's eyes warmed as he squeezed her hands, prompting her heart-beat to skip and skip and skip.

~

a few minutes later, she slipped out of the back door with Luca and walked with him to the edge of the estate. Pulko bid her farewell and began the journey to Colchester, with the assurance that Luca would join him shortly.

The morning was chilly and blustery and Luca pulled on his black leather hawking gloves. She stood with him in a field of new meadow grass, on the trimming of the rusty pond overlooking the crofter's cottage. Luca had placed two stone urns flanking the doorway of the cottage and replaced the thatched roof. He'd promised to fill the urns with violets when the weather turned warmer. Another sign that he'd return.

Looking every bit the Gypsy, Luca tied his orange scarf around his hair, his ruby ring glinting from his forefinger. His cloak was slung over one shoulder, the patch of rabbit fur sewn securely to one sleeve. His swarthy complexion glowed robust and healthier than he'd looked in weeks.

He caught her in his arms and locked his lips to hers. She slid her hands over the familiar black bristle of his beard and rested her palms against his chest. His heart pounded beneath her fingertips, reaching inside her to a secret, heart-breaking place.

"Don't forget to change your bandages. I packed you several clean cloths. And please, be safe," she said.

Grinning, he patted his pouch, filled with linen cloths, sliced brown bread, and a favorite Bible verse she'd written on a sheet of paper.

Romans 12:12: *Be joyful in hope, patient in affliction, faithful in prayer*.

She shivered in the bitter breeze and he secured her pelisse snugly to her chin. It was these thoughtful acts, a gentleman concerned about his lady's comfort, all the reasons why she cared so much for him.

He neared the woods, his strides devouring the ground. His limp was slight. Several times, he walked backward and gave an exuberant wave. He was hindered by his injury but she never doubted his deftness. With chiseled features and a stubborn, angled chin, he was a man riddled in complexities and strange customs and never-ending duties.

And with each passing day, she was realizing more and more that he was the man who completed her.

When he assumed she no longer saw him, his gait slowed, his limp more distinct. In the harsh daylight, in the harsh breeze, he tried to hide it from her, the fact that his leg hadn't completely healed. When he was in pain, and she knew he always was, he disguised it under an indulgent grin and nonchalant shrug.

She swung from the woodlands and shuffled to the dower house. Determinedly, she blinked through a pall of unshed tears. Desolation spilled like a virus, taking hold, until she stopped to take great gulps of cold air. The clean, cutting snap of wind reminded her that winter still held a grip on the land.

How could she survive a day without him, let alone a fortnight? He was a man of principles, of obligations, she reminded herself, and she'd await his return proudly, patiently.

She fastened the belt around her pelisse and increased her pace to the house.

A stack of mending filled her basket that she'd neglected since his arrival. Better to keep her fingers busy throughout the long, lonely days.

CHAPTER EIGHTEEN

*S*everal hours after Luca and Pulko had departed, Patience retired to her bedchamber for an afternoon nap. She hadn't meant to glance out her bedchamber's window when she awoke. She was simply walking from her closet to the bed, deciding on which frock to wear the following day. Black mourning clothes, perhaps with a green satin bow beneath her mob cap to contain her unruly waves.

Tawny sunlight crisscrossed the bed hangings, heralding the onset of evening.

A cold breeze came through the window, apparently left ajar by one of the servants. She walked to the window and decided to leave it open for a few minutes. The breeze freshened the stale air of a long winter.

The sun set quickly, encircled in one last bright hue of yellow, although a crack of thunder boomed in the distance. She sniffed. Rain was in the air.

Penham trimmed the lamps and lit the torch lights. Gazing at the flickering fires, she pondered how English society would view her relationship with a Gypsy, if and when she was found innocent of Crispin's murder conviction. Most likely, the English would look at Luca with pronounced disdain and distaste.

She went back to her wardrobe, stopping to light two beeswax candles from the dwindling ashes in the fireplace. She set the candles on the mantel and wiped the blurriness from her eyes. She'd been exhausted from her walk to the croft cottage with Luca to see him off and had hoped that a nap would refresh her. Instead, her brain was foggy and she felt light-headed.

Thinking of Luca again, she smiled. A Gypsy artist. A good man. An honorable man, conflicted by his responsibilities. He'd said that he'd return to visit her whenever he could, and to call upon a *vurma* to summon him if Patience suspected she was in any danger.

The flickering lights of the candles warmed her with a quiet thankfulness. Tonight, she'd enjoy a good meal and sleep soundly.

She washed leisurely and pulled a clean black frock over her head, debating whether to call for Amelia's help to button the small pearl buttons at the top of the neckline.

A noise outside her window, the crunch of unfamiliar footsteps starting and stopping, caused her to pause. The servants scurried downstairs from kitchen to dining room, making last-minute dinner preparations. Lamb cutlets, fresh green vegetables, and thick sweet strawberry pudding for dessert made Patience's mouth water. Her appetite, thankfully, hadn't been deterred by her tiredness.

Unfamiliar footsteps outside. Again?

Her hands stopped at her throat. Perhaps Marko and his men watched her dower house all this time, giving her a false sense of safety, all the while planning an attack.

She grabbed one of the candles on the mantel, hurried to the tall bedchamber window, and peered out. Dusky shadows had turned the sky to black and the wind had picked up. Her white sheer curtains billowed outward, sucked through the open space of the window.

She set the candle on the wardrobe and grabbed the sash, intending to close the window before rain left puddles on the wood floor.

There. Near the trees. A blinding flash of lightning lit the ground. A large man with a stringy black beard stood beneath a row of hedges. He mopped his forehead with a rumpled handkerchief, his demeanor dark and menacing.

She froze. Heavy rains slit against the window pane. She shoved the window down, too shocked to move away. Her heart thudded madly. She jerked against the wall and pressed a hand to her chest. A Gypsy man. He looked like Marko, but she couldn't be sure.

She drew to the side of the window and carefully lifted the curtains to peer out.

Perhaps she was still dreaming from her earlier nap, for Luca had scoured the fields endless times and assured her that Marko was nowhere in sight and probably had gone back to his caravan weeks before.

Thunder rattled the windowpane. Lightning flared.

Through a blur of white sheer curtains and blinding rain, the large man raised a fist at her.

She gasped and jerked back from the window, her hands clutching the curtains.

She gathered her breath and peered out, one more time. Surely no one was there.

And no one was.

A scant few hours earlier, Luca had instructed her. 'If you need me, send Penham. He'll find the vurma on the cattle path along the sea and she can direct him to my tribe's camp.'

Nay. After spending so many days with Patience, Luca had only just begun his long journey back to his tribe. They needed him. Fabiana needed him. He'd been away too long.

Patience pressed her lips together. She refused to interrupt him within a few hours of his departure because of her wild imagination, showing herself as a pitiable, needy, dependent woman who couldn't last one day without him.

She lifted the curtains, one last time.

Aye, just as she'd thought. She'd imagined Marko.

CHAPTER NINETEEN

Two days afterward, Luca arrived in Colchester. Pulko had gone on ahead. Evening neared, and an exuberant chorus of exclamations from his tribe greeted him as he approached. The teeming scents of timber fires and crackling meats drew him to the center of the camp.

"*Misto*! Welcome!" Fabiana hailed.

"You're apparently feeling better," Luca observed.

Fabiana waved a dismissive hand at herself. "All I needed was rest and some good, fresh fish." She eyed Luca warily and kept a scrupulous frown on his limp. "Did your fine countess and her hard-working maid fix your leg properly this time?"

"Properly and completely," Luca prevaricated. "And Pulko found us food along the way and made a *bender* for us to sleep at night while we traveled. He took good care of me. Your son will become a fine Roma lord someday."

"'Tis too much responsibility for a boy so young."

"He's older than I was when I became a lord." Luca looked around. "And where is this boy who's like a *plal*, a brother, to me? I couldn't keep up with him."

Fabiana grinned. "He returned a couple of hours ago.

Presently, he's stealing from a noble who owns far too many horses. Pulko is taking a chestnut mare off the *gadje's* hands as we speak. *Yekka buliasa nashti beshes pe done grastende*."

Luca translated in English, "With one behind you cannot sit on two horses." He strode to his *bender* and Fabiana's voice followed him.

"The *gadje* are greedy and selfish," she said.

Proud of her Romany heritage—speaking from seasoned knowledge regarding the despised *gadje*—the always practical and ever opinionated Fabiana never kept her views on life to herself.

Luca rested on a log near the campfire and stretched out his legs. "Are you referring to any *gadje* in particular, Fabiana?"

"Aye. Your fancy English countess." Fabiana tromped through the sand, carefully avoiding the marsh orchids, and lingered near the campfire. "How many days will you remain with us before you return to her?"

"How many days, weeks, years, do you expect me to stay before my debt to the tribe is repaid? I appreciate that you raised me and cared for my mother when she was ill, but now I'm a man with other interests."

"Other interests besides your duties?" Fabiana peered up at the sky, her countenance forbidding, as though she appealed to the heavens for guidance on how to steer an unruly, unappreciative child who'd insisted on giving the wrong answer.

"Have I not cared for the tribe since I was little more than a boy?" Luca persisted.

"Aye, and with no complaint until now. But don't play the long-suffering martyr, for Pulko has kept us abreast of your growing attraction to Lady Blakwell."

Luca rubbed his jaw and gazed at a flock of gulls screeching overhead. "You speak of my interest as if it were a hideous crime."

"The English nobles refuse to help the Rom and they attack without an excuse. They won't spare so much as a coin, even when we starve and beg for work. Can you not recall how much your mother suffered, all because she loved an Englishman? The Rom helped her when she was alone and birthed two sons. Where were the English? Where was your father?"

"How can I ever forget? You've reminded me a thousand times."

"Are the Rom, your people, an obligation now that you've gotten a taste of a grander life? A duty you want to rid yourself of as quickly as possible?"

He trained his stare on the wet leaves and twigs scattered in the sand.

Fabiana twisted her fingers through the fringe of her bright pink shawl. "Nadya has healed, and the scars on her face from Marko's thrashings are noticeable only on her forehead, which she hides with her beautiful long hair."

Luca didn't glance at Fabiana. There was no need to see her expression, for he felt certain it was grudgingly pleasant now that she spoke about a Romany woman.

"Nadya wanted me to send word when you arrived," Fabiana continued. "Will you see her?"

"Of course," Luca agreed. "But first, I'll meet with Pulko to discuss our provisions."

As if on cue, Pulko appeared at the edge of the camp, sliding on a slick patch of muddy grass and landing at Luca's feet. Despite the mud streaming down his face, Pulko raised two cackling chickens for the tribesmen to admire.

"Are you not a clever thief?" Luca laughed. "You go to steal a horse and come back with two chickens."

Fabiana scooped the chickens and Pulko hoisted himself to his feet.

"I'll steal the horse come the morrow," Pulko said. "The chickens will feed us tonight."

"Aye, along with the pantry provisions furnished by Lady Blakwell," Luca said.

Two spots of bright red appeared on Pulko's whiskered cheeks. He swiped the mud and jutted his chin, looking for all the world like he'd been grievously misunderstood. "The elders needed food."

Luca restrained a grin as he peered into Pulko's fire-breathing eyes. "'Tis a habit of yours of late," he couldn't resist baiting. "Whenever you see me, you carry fowl in your hands."

Later in the evening, Luca took a place with the elders in the marshy grass by the sea. A comet streamed across the black sky, its tail shimmering. The men put down their tambourines and waited for the comet to pass. Luca knew Fabiana would predict the event as a bad omen.

He stretched out on the grass, feeling the salty air on his face, tasting it on his lips.

Black pepper and garlic sizzled from a pot over the campfire, and several women roasted the two charred chickens on a spit. Crisp green beans simmered in a vegetable broth. Fried bacon flavored the air. Some of the old men and women jangled tambourines and sang in the familiar Romanes language, sparked by a tinge of Indian and English accents.

Withdrawing paper and a pen from his cloak, Luca sketched the scene—a scene he'd observed hundreds of times. Through the years he'd accumulated stacks of sketches from his nomadic life, the everyday trials of his tribe, the little he remembered of his slim, dark-skinned mother. One of his sketches was her standing beside their crude tent. She held a gleaming gold bird cage and gazed fondly at the tiny brown finch perched on a stick in the cage. The bird chirped and trilled and she'd laughed aloud.

'There's such beauty in this world,' she'd said.

But she didn't live in this world anymore, and nothing was gleaming and gold, and no brown finch trilled, because there was no paradise for a ragged tribe. Only stark reality and the need to survive.

His sketches were just that, sketches, and each sentimentalized his harsh existence beneath muted lines and caring portrayals, renderings that left streaks of longing whenever he contemplated leaving the tribe to find a life for himself. Scents of his childhood, bergamot and roses, tender and hopeful, jumbled with the pointed smell of his loss when his mother had died.

Luca glanced up as a stunning ebony-haired Roma woman approached. She drew a bright green cloak across her shoulders. A plum-striped *diklo*, handkerchief, was tied at her throat. She flipped back her heavy black hair, and large, gold hoop earrings flashed from her ears.

Luca placed the paper on the ground and stood. "Nadya, you're looking well," he said.

"As are you, my friend." She studied him with eagerness, the look she used whenever gazing at a man. "You always look well." Nadya licked her lips and pushed the band of silver bracelets up her arms.

"All these compliments," he mused. "I don't know how to respond."

He expected her to rejoin with an innuendo, for he'd played her flirting game for years.

She remained quiet, a modest concession for all they'd been through. He was silent, also. Perhaps their long-ago attraction and the resulting violence had humbled them both.

Bending slightly, she studied his sketch, purposely allowing an unobstructed view of her loose bodice. He shook his head and smiled. She hadn't changed.

But he had.

As she straightened, Luca wrapped her cloak tighter around her shoulders and secured the laces at the neckline. "'Tis a cold night," he said, an excuse for an explanation.

She granted him an appreciative smile adorned in provocation. "My new husband has vowed to defend me if Marko ever comes near me."

"Aye, congratulations on your marriage. Where is your new husband this evening?"

"He's probably sleeping." She shrugged. "And I heard that your tribe was recently attacked by the English."

"Trouble-making English men wanting to bring danger and sadness to the Rom," Luca replied. "'Tis always their way."

"The memories of your merciless beating at Marko's hands haunt me still." Nadya took a long breath and fiddled with the sleeves of her cloak. "Luca, I know that if you'd realized that Marko was going to beat me that night after you got away, you would've stayed and tried to protect me. I wanted to give you more food..."

Luca nodded. A pain shot up his leg, a ruthless reminder, although she'd suffered as well. She was a flirt, knowing no other course other than bartering herself for survival. But once, long ago, he'd cared for her. And, in her own way, she'd cared for him.

She shivered. "There's a wind by the sea. Can we speak in your *bender*?"

Once they were inside, Luca lit a candle and set it on a rough table. The flicker of candlelight changed Nadya's slanted eyes to the slit, reflective eyes of a cat.

He poured them both a cup of weak, cold tea. "*Sastimos*." He raised his cup. "Good health."

"*Sastimos*."

He leaned against the timbered pole holding up the middle of his tent and observed her. Her honey brown features were striking, although a hardness around her lips and eyes had claimed her former beauty.

"Fabiana and Pulko said you plan to visit the countess's estate again," Nadya said. "Why are you pursuing this woman?"

She asked the question politely. Nevertheless, her voice was too shrill, and he saw the question for what it was—an inquisition, the beginning of a series of interrogations about his life and plans, for which he had no answers because his loyalties to both Patience and his tribe were tearing him apart.

He sipped his tea ever so casually. "Why indeed? The countess saved my life."

Nadya spat into her cup and wiped her mouth with her hand. "Because she saved your life, must you give your life in return and abandon the Rom?"

"I'm not abandoning anyone." His jaw tightened. He tried to keep his tone cool.

"From what I've heard, she's a plain dowager widow. I know you." Nadya's voice lowered. "I know what you like."

"Then surely you don't think you can force me to declare my intentions."

Nadya tossed her cup to the floor. "Let me know when you tire of her." She glanced at his hawking gloves set on his pallet. "May I take these? Since my beating, I cannot stay warm."

"Of course. They were never mine to begin with."

Her long fingernail grazed the fur and traced the embroidered gold initials. "Whose markings are these?"

"Most likely some rich English dandy," Luca replied.

~

*S*everal weeks passed.

Luca lifted his head from the task of skinning the rabbit he'd caught earlier in the day. It was the second time that he'd heard a man's cries for help by the river near the sea. It couldn't be Nanosh's voice, for he rarely left Marko's side, although the voice sounded like his.

An icy breeze, a draconian breath, stormed across Luca's nape. He grabbed his walking stick and hurried toward the shout and the river beyond. The crunchity-crunch of gravel crushed beneath his boots as he reached the river's edge. Violent, cloudy water glutted the embankment.

He spotted Nanosh, a speck of flailing hands and dark hair. Waves pooled around his neck as the current drove him swiftly downstream.

Luca's blood hammered in pulse-stopping panic. He'd never seen Nanosh helpless before. Even when they were children, Nanosh was always the most daring.

"Nanosh! Keep your head up!" Luca shouted.

Water rushed between the rocks, flowed toward the waterfalls, thrusting Nanosh ever farther out of reach. Not daring to look away, Luca darted with the current. He stretched his walking stick over the water. "Here! Reach for this!"

Nanosh thrashed against the raging upsurge and made an attempt to grab the walking stick. Then he disappeared beneath a churning river that didn't care.

An unaccustomed moment of fright swept through Luca. He couldn't swim. And neither could Nanosh. The Rom never had a reason to swim, as they roamed the land, not the sea.

Nanosh thrashed against the raging upsurge and made a frantic attempt to grab the walking stick.

"Dear God," Luca flung his walking stick to the ground. "I

know this man is my enemy but I need to help him." Without another thought, he tore off his cloak. Feet braced, arms outstretched, he plunged into the unforgiving depths. Icy water rose to his neck. The waves pushed him downward. He clawed at the soaked hair in his eyes. He had to breathe, had to overcome his fear.

From beneath the muddy water, Nanosh's shouts of panic echoed. He came to the surface, his mouth distorted, his expression torturous. All color drained from his face. Then he disappeared.

Luca no longer saw the cruel adult man with the pot belly. He remembered the skinny Romany boy, fresh-faced and adventurous, playing mischievous tricks on the other boys.

"Where are you?" Luca's cries labored across the river.

The river opened into a pool and the current flowed weaker.

Luca took a deep breath and dove under. Crests of water, smelling of fish, roiled to his chin. Never had he been so powerless to save someone.

He pushed to the surface and saw Pulko extending his arms. "I'll help you."

Nanosh came up beside Luca, his intake of breath guttural. Pulko pulled both Luca and Nanosh to the river-bank. Then he towed Nanosh's heavy, leaden body to dryer land.

Luca braced his arms against the ground and dragged air into his lungs. Half-crawling, he reached Nanosh. Nanosh's head lolled to the side. His black hair clung to his pale face.

"Is he dead?" Pulko asked.

Luca rose to his knees. "Nay." He placed his ear against his mouth. "He's taken in water, but he's breathing."

"He shouldn't have been near our camp," Pulko said.

"As children, we were all friends." Luca placed his hands

on Nanosh's ribcage and bore down. Water spurted from Nanosh's mouth. He coughed and sputtered.

"Why are you here, prowling near our tribe?" Pulko shouted at Nanosh.

"Marko wants Luca dead." Nanosh directed his black-eyed glare at Luca. "Did you save me so that you can slice me to pieces?"

"I saved you so that you'd live." Luca glanced at Pulko. "We both did."

"I'll return when Marko commands."

"And if you return and slip into the river again, I'll save you again." Luca came to his feet and grabbed his walking stick. The foul smell of the river clung to the insides of his nose and throat. Coarse silt stuck to the roof of his mouth. His waterlogged clothes chafed against his cold skin.

Luca and Pulko walked away from Nanosh in silence. Luca heard Nanosh's footsteps as he headed into the forest.

After a few moments, Pulko said, "You cannot swim."

"Aye," Luca said.

Unashamed respect shone in Pulko's eyes as he looked up at Luca. "Nevertheless, you dove into the river to save your worst enemy."

"Aye." Luca stared straight ahead at the tattered tents of his tribe. "Because nothing is more important than keeping peace and ensuring the safety of those we love."

Love. Luca shook his head. The thought had just come. Had it sat there idly, all this time, waiting for the right moment to admit how much he cared for Patience?

"I'm returning to Lady Blakwell's estate." He couldn't control the tremor in his voice.

Patience had made him a better man. And he needed to be with her.

CHAPTER TWENTY

*O*liver gave a gruff growl.

Patience jolted up in bed. She rubbed her eyes and squinted into the stark darkness of her bedchamber. Streaks of jagged lightning glistered through the cracks in the window, followed by a thunderclap. Strange weather for late winter, perhaps a hint of spring. With God's grace, Luca was safely with his tribe. Although he was far away, he continued to occupy her thoughts.

She reached to her night table. Even in the dark, she made out the bold lines of the sketch he'd drawn of her. He was naturally talented, his detail painstaking. Several weeks had gone by since his departure, however the hollowness, the empty sadness in her chest by his absence, persisted.

His gift had been heartfelt and genuine. She hadn't fully realized, nor fully appreciated, his sincerity. Now it was too late to tell him for he was no longer here and she didn't know when he'd return.

A gust of cold air rushed through her room, bringing her musings to the present. With great care, Patience tied the sketch in a blue silk ribbon and placed it in the top drawer of her night table.

She stared at her bedchamber door, securely bolted. The windows were sealed. The chilly gray of an early spring's dawn was hours away, permitting her a few more hours of sleep. Deeply, she inhaled. The scent of lavender soap, soothing and floral, lingered on her skin from her wash.

She tucked her knee-length night dress closer to her body and snuggled beneath thick woolen blankets. Sleep was what she needed to stave off the constant tiredness assailing her. She curved her head into the feather pillow. Just as she drifted off, the tinkling of a pianoforte interrupted her dreams of a dashing, black-eyed Gypsy. She fought off the luring sensation of slumber and opened her eyes.

Somewhere in the house a floorboard groaned, deadened but distinctive. She propped on her elbows, found her breath, and swallowed. No one came in the black of night, although she swore the heavy entry door had creaked open.

Her gaze darted across her bedchamber. Something didn't feel right.

Hackles raised, ears high, Oliver leapt to the door and emitted one low growl. Patience calmed her quick heartbeat and lurched to her feet. Her head whirled and she sat on the edge of the bed to stop the dizziness. Fumbling in the darkness, she shoved her arms through the sleeves of her morning gown and wrapped a warm cashmere shawl about her shoulders.

She flattened her body close to Oliver and pressed her ear to the door. The familiar voice of her stepson singing off-key coasted through the hallway, along with the eerie finality of a C Minor chord.

"Stay here," she whispered to Oliver. She unfastened the door latch and padded down the wooden stairway. Rounding the corner of the dining room, she searched the shadowed length of the drawing room. A fire burned low in the fireplace. Her step-son, Crispin, occupied the bench in front of the pianoforte, his head lowered over the keys, his wine glass clutched in one hand. The smell of port wine and expensive cologne burdened the air.

She knotted the shawl around her shoulders and waited.

He was here for something. She wasn't sure what, or why, but it had nothing to do with perfecting the coda of a Haydn Sonatina. His loud and wheezy breathing reeked of vengeance, and money, and blackmail.

"Your pianoforte recital in the middle of the night woke me. Now that you're finished, I'll light more candles so you can see the keys," she said.

Crispin whipped his head up. "Leave them unlit. Beeswax is expensive." He scraped the bench back, stood, and grasped the pianoforte fallboard before weaving his way to the dining room.

His white linen shirt was opened at the neck and exposed a square jaw that reminded her of a lantern. His waistcoat hung undone.

He used his height to his advantage and squinted down at her. "Shall I bid a good evening to the woman who murdered my father?"

Wine reeked from his skin and she debated answering, afraid to edge him on, reluctant to draw back. "Your accusations are untrue, as you certainly know."

"Several months ago, you plotted my father's murder. Were you so desperate to be rid of him that you assumed I'd ignore our English law?" Unblinking, his peculiarly small eyes were unnerving.

He was a strange, unpredictable man, playing the pianoforte softly when he thought no one watched, because men usually didn't play the pianoforte. Then slamming at the keys when he played a passage poorly, therefore making a loud display of that which he'd tried to hide a moment before.

"Digby found my father lying unconscious in this very house, completely alone the night he died. Perhaps you hired a bandit to beat my father senseless, then fled from the crime," Crispin continued.

"All lies," she replied. If he hadn't watched her so closely, she might have surrendered to her fatigue and sunk onto a side chair. However, a sign of fragility wasn't a trait she wanted to show a calculating creature like him.

Crispin staggered to a mahogany sideboard and topped off his wine glass. "You were the last person to speak to my father."

"Actually, Digby was the last person," she countered. "On the afternoon of your visit, your father had said he was too busy to see you because of some budgetary work, but I persuaded him to make time for you. The day followed Epiphany, because I remember saying special prayers before I took my dog for a walk."

She didn't add that she'd purposely arranged her walk to avoid her stepson's arrival, as she had no desire to share a meal under his and his father's lecherous scrutiny.

"A convenient excuse as to your whereabouts," Crispin said. "However, no one saw you or your tiny dog anywhere in the village that day."

She waited until he drank another mouthful of wine. "The path I take is often deserted. I prefer the solitude."

"I suspect you met your lover." Crispin quaffed his wine, choked on a mouthful, and spit into his glass. "Is he the mysterious Gypsy the footmen whispered about when they greeted me this evening?"

She crossed her arms. "I have nothing to hide."

He regarded her, his small eyes as frozen as the Thames in January. "Gypsies are backward and primitive, more suited to rat-catching and fortune-telling than actual work. Or did he dance and play his fiddle for you?"

"How can you speak so callously of an entire race of people simply because you don't understand their way of life?" Her blood surged, the breath hot in her throat. Crispin's views were narrow-minded and intolerant, but she didn't want to raise his suspicions by speaking further and perhaps placing Luca in danger.

She shot a glance toward the large glass window. Outdoors, the fields lightened with the emergence of a full moon, brightening the starkness of the room.

"However, at present my interest is finding my father's murderer," Crispin said. "Some servants spoke of my father's roughness with you. Some said they heard muffled screams from your bedchamber when he visited you late in the evening. You wanted him dead, didn't you?"

Her mouth dried. Despite her poorly concealed shudder whenever her husband had touched her, he'd treated her cordially in public. Seldom had they openly quarreled. To the outsider, she seemed an ideal wife, docile, genteel, and all that English society expected.

Of course, she scarcely tolerated the sight of him and her feelings must've shown. And because he knew, he'd used the knowledge to his advantage, taunting her all the more, confident he held all the control. She bore his clammy hands, his smell of vinegar and roiled charcoal when he placed his arms possessively over her shoulders and kissed her with an open mouth.

She lowered her eyes. She was supposed to have loved her husband, not loathe him.

Her inner chastisements were drowned by Crispin's slurred voice. "Heeding your instructions, Digby added ground ginger to father's medicine to ease his discomfort. I believe you disguised a toxic herb in the ginger to finish your cold-hearted deed."

Patience headed for the hallway. "I refuse to listen."

Crispin wound his way around the dining table, his silhouette in the candlelight crisscrossing hers. "Did you make good use of the money I sent last month?"

Although she bore the expense and burden of keeping the ledgers and paying the servants on less than half of what was needed, Crispin was the heir and he controlled the money.

She stared at him, dressed like a dandy with his gold-buttoned frockcoat, his pointed top hat sitting on the dining table next to his glass of port wine. He always dressed in the latest fashions, trying to show off to anyone who cared to look.

His father, her late husband, had never seemed impressed.

She put a fist over her mouth in her best imitation of a yawn. "We can speak about money in the morning."

She should've departed, and would have, if Crispin hadn't leaned on the dining room table and drummed his fingers in a repetitive, grating rhythm. When he seemed certain he had her attention, he withdrew a stack of paper from his waistcoat and placed them on the table. "If I formally accuse you in court of murdering your husband, a nobleman, and you're found guilty, you'll be charged with petty treason."

"I'm well aware of this."

"The prison you'll be going to will be much worse than debtor's prison."

His cool monotone made her veins drone with an apprehension that filled her ears.

"You cannot withhold one-third of my dower on speculation," she said. "I was a faithful and dutiful wife and your false claims will be scoffed out of court."

"The court won't side with a woman without any family to speak of, and little land to call her own."

"I can plead 'privilege of peerage.'"

"Not for a murder charge." Crispin shook his head, then smiled. "Fortunately for you, I've decided on a satisfactory solution. You'll come and live with me in Mayfair. After all, you're my stepmother."

Her wits went utterly blank. Her legs weakened. "I'll not leave Ipswich and Amelia."

Crispin scrutinized her body at leisure, deliberately insulting. "We'll reside in father's London townhouse. You'll do my bidding and I'll not charge you with murder."

He spoke in vain, for she no longer listened. The drone in her ears vibrated to a howling roar. "Your father drew up a pre-contract with my father," she said. "The terms of my dower rights are clear, as well as the amount agreed upon for my living expenses."

"Money is of no benefit if your future is standing in front of a firing squad." Deep scars blighted Crispin's cheeks as he leered toward her. Her skin pricked and her pulse slowed to a repugnant crawl.

"Never will I live with my late husband's son in the manner you infer," she said.

"You'll consent when you realize that if you don't, you'll lose any remaining wealth, your freedom, and possibly your life."

She felt nauseated. She couldn't swallow. Whirling, she clutched her restless fingers into the creases of her shawl and stormed up the stairwell.

CHAPTER TWENTY-ONE

*L*uca could no longer contain his impatience. He missed Patience more than he could bear and needed to see her. For several long weeks, he'd fished and hunted with Pulko, cod, rabbits, and small game, ensuring the tribe had enough food for the sennights ahead. He'd done enough.

Later that day, when the sun settled low in the sky, Luca grabbed some clean clothes, slid his pouch over his shoulder, and told the tribe of his decision. He was returning to Patience for good.

"We'll starve," Pulko objected. "You'll grow bored and fat and idle and—"

"Pulko, with each passing day I believe that you're a better leader than I am. You're much quicker and have shown yourself to be brave. Besides, I'll be near enough if you need me." Luca grabbed his cloak and slung it over his shoulders.

On foot, the journey would take a couple of days. He bid the tribe an abrupt farewell and headed out of camp.

After hours of traipsing a sandy footpath, thirst and

hunger slowed Luca's movements. He hadn't eaten, insistent on saving every bit of food for the tribe.

True, the tribe had provisions, salted and pickled for the days ahead, but food went bad quickly as the weather got warmer. Besides, he planned to feast when he reached Patience's dower house. Amelia was surely simmering a miniature pastry filled with beef marrow, followed by sweet jellies on toast. He grinned. He was beginning to relish English pound cake topped with clotted cream more than a Romany roasted hedgehog dredged in black pepper.

He paused and drank some black tea from a flagon in his pouch.

The past few fortnights had worn on him with tribal tasks and disputes needing prompt, undistracted attention and he'd gotten little sleep. Perhaps he should've waited until morning, but he was anxious to see Patience before another day broke. Besides, he was used to covering ground at dark and blending with the forest.

He let out a moan as pain shot through his leg. Rest, he thought, but he rejected the thought as a waste of precious time. The flat footpath was the longer route to Patience's house. Hiking up the hills was the shorter route, but hills were difficult to navigate with a limp and put undue strain on his bad leg. And he refused to use any wretched tree branch as a walking stick.

Familiar twinges of the muscles burning his calf became a grating agony. He strained on, already feeling the tightening in his thigh.

Tormenting, torturous suffering from a damn gouge refusing to properly and completely heal.

He pulled his orange handkerchief from his head, wiped his brow, then retied the knot around his hair. His limp slowed to faltering footsteps, but each faltering footstep brought him one step closer to Patience.

~

*A*lmost midnight. He should stop. Sleep.

Patience would be the first to tell him thus, worried for him, chiding him for driving himself too far, too long. But he refused to be beaten by any wretched discomfort, for it meant physical pain had won, and his inner drive had lost.

Hour by hour, the clouds grew lower, and denser, and bleaker, marking the hours before dawn. The craggy hills loomed around, behind, ahead.

Luca pictured himself when he was nine and twenty, when he was fit and able. Running, hiking, climbing. He was only a year older now. Of course he could climb a steep hill. What was simpler than climbing a steep, craggy hill?

He switched his path and determinedly approached the incline.

Think in small steps. Focus.

Weak leg, strong leg, weak leg, strong leg. He paced himself, placing one foot in front of the other, scrambling up the sudden bends, grabbing slender tree trunks to steady himself. If he slowed to a creep, the spasms in his calf were bearable, although that meant a journey of two days would stretch to three. Indeed, three days could stretch to four.

His pouch hung loose from his shoulder as he climbed. The scarf around his hair worked from the knot and sweat pooled down his neck, lingering in a salty line. He shaded his eyes and peered at the peak soaring above.

Surely the peak was unreachable.

The thought, utterly defeating, lowered him to his knees. It hadn't seemed difficult when he'd had Pulko on the journey to help him.

He yanked off his cloak and rubbed the rabbit fur sewn to his cloak sleeve, smoothing the softness against his face. In the past, he'd believed that rabbit fur brought good luck. Now he knew better. The Rom's superstitions were just that. Superstitions.

He peered at the top of the hill and blinked to clear the shadows. He shook his head, knowing the shadows were phantoms of his own fatigue. Shakily, he stood and stepped hard to avoid a large stone in his path, laying all his weight on his injured leg.

He took a sharp breath. His leg caved. He slipped to the ground and cursed.

Forget the agony. It will pass. He needed to reach Patience because he loved her. Aye, he was bone-deep in love. And she loved him. He knew it, felt it. They needed to be together.

He offered a prayer to her Christian God in his Romany tongue.

Then he pushed himself to his feet and kept walking.

CHAPTER TWENTY-TWO

*L*uca arrived at Patience's dower house just before noon on his third day of travel. He passed a row of primrose on the last curving lane and waved away a swarm of wasps clumped atop a neglected jam pot. Already it was the beginning of May. Soon, yellow wildflowers would carpet the fields, filling the air with the light, lemony fragrance that reminded him of spring.

Keeping himself hidden behind the hedges, his boots scuffed the gravel along a side pathway leading to the back kitchen entrance. He knew the layout of the house so well he could walk it blindfolded.

Oliver danced a greeting at the doorway. The dog flung to his back for a stomach rub, then scampered around Luca. Amelia flattened pastry dough on a wooden table in the kitchen as Luca rapped on the door and entered. Penham stood across from her, slicing green apples and fresh almonds. A pot of vinegar boiled on the stove.

"Leave the dog outside." Amelia wiped a floury hand across her hair, and met Luca's gaze. She gaped. Her eyes bulged. "God alive, Mr. Gypsy, I thought you were the stable man. From the corner of my eye, your clothes resembled little more than rags."

"Thank you," Luca replied dryly. "You're looking well, also."

With a pat on his thigh to Oliver, he let the dog into the field. He closed the door and set his pouch and walking stick on a side table. He wended to Penham's side of the kitchen and was met by the man's condemning scowl. "It took you a long time to return," the man observed.

"Did you and Pulko manage to do any stealing in Colchester?" Amelia clapped her hand over her mouth, seemingly horrified at the audacity of her own question.

Luca's lips twitched. "Stealing isn't an occupation for a Rom so much as a necessity. Aye, Pulko stole chickens and a horse while I hunted."

Amelia's plump fingers went back to shaping the dough into a crust. Penham set the sliced apples in a crock on the side table and grabbed an apple slice. Amelia's rolling pin flew out to whack his hand, her pastry crust apparently forgotten.

"Those apples are for the tartes, you overgrown servant." Amelia lambasted him with an exasperated look and made an about-face to Luca, granting him a broad smile. "Lady Blakwell has awaited your arrival on tenterhooks when several fortnights passed with no word from you. She fretted you were waylaid."

"I was, by hunting, and fishing, and Rom disputes, and this accursed leg—" Luca snuck a slice of apple, expecting to meet a whack from Amelia's rolling pin, but she radiated her consent.

"I could use more of your special liniment," he said.

Amelia reached into a cupboard and handed him a vial.

"Thank you." Luca took another slice of apple and scrutinized the kitchen. "Where's my beautiful countess?"

"She's in the dining room contemplating a journey," Amelia averred.

"What journey?"

Amelia wrung her hands and gave Luca a pained stare. "Lady Blakwell will soon be journeying to London to live with her stepson, Lord Crispin. He's coerced her into going or he'll charge her formally in court with his father's murder. 'Tis disgraceful. He's five and twenty and has left her with no choice." Amelia moved about, seeming unable to stay in one place. "'Twill be safer for us all if you leave."

"I'm staying." Luca's voice hardened. He felt a rock taking a firm place in his throat when he tried to swallow. "And don't try to stop me."

"Ssh." With a quick glance over her shoulder and a sound thrust at his chest, Amelia handed Luca his walking stick and sent Luca in reverse. "Penham has chores to finish in the basement, and you need to go outside and hide. 'Tis safer because Crispin's in the drawing room." She banged the door shut.

Luca stood, grasping his walking stick, a Roma man standing in an Englishwoman's garden. Then he eased the door open, slipped into the pantry, and flattened himself against the shelves.

The playing of a Scottish Air on the pianoforte in the drawing room was followed by a gruff male voice. "Who's here, Amelia?"

Luca's eyebrows shot up. Sifting through hazy memories, he recognized the man.

He straightened from the shelves and crouched in the half-open doorway of the pantry, absently petting an orange tabby at his heels. He peered through the doorway and into the drawing room beyond to make certain that the man's face connected to the voice.

Aye, it was the same man, although Luca hadn't known

Crispin's name until now. Crispin seated at the pianoforte. He had the same pitted cheeks and lunging nose.

Sickening remembrances surged in Luca's mind. The twelve-year-old Roma girl had been beaten beyond recognition. Crispin had towered over her, guilty, although proclaiming innocence in a high-pitched whine. The stench of her unwashed blood had contaminated the tender green field. The odor of brutality permeated the air.

Luca pushed down the blind fury rising in his chest. He hadn't been able to save her. He'd been too late. Somehow, he quelled the urge to tear into the drawing room and demand justice from the man, the nobleman, who'd deemed himself above the law.

The minutes passed. Fragments of conversation between Amelia and Crispin went by in a drone of faceless voices and a final, crashing pianoforte chord.

"Lord Crispin, perhaps a promenade down the lane will lighten your sour mood?" Amelia asked. "Here's your cloak and top hat," she added gaily. "I'll have your carriage sent round."

When the front entry was secured, Luca bypassed any idle conversation with Amelia and razed a glare toward the front entry. "I know that man and I loathe him."

"There's an air of cruelty about Lord Crispin that chills my brittle bones. He reminds me of his late father, although they never got along." Amelia muttered under her breath, then paused. "Why do you loathe him?"

Luca's jaw tensed, his mind in conflict. Looking back to that terrible day, he felt Crispin's viciousness overtaking the cold spring air, leashed below politeness, contained beneath civility. He wanted to expose Crispin for what he was and wrench off the fur-lined frock cloak shielding the vicious nobleman underneath.

"A long time ago, a young Roma girl bled at Crispin's feet."

Luca sighed heavily, spoke quieter. "Behind his silky tongue hides a violent nature."

"What happened?" Amelia asked.

"The girl he murdered was from a neighboring tribe, and word spread quickly, but Crispin spouted drunken denials when her brothers demanded justice because he knew the courts were on his side." Luca wearily rubbed his leg, the ache beginning to rage through his calf. "No one was there to prove otherwise, and it was an English noble's word against a dead Roma girl. Perhaps she'd tried to sell her body—for food or a warm place to sleep. Her tribe was too afraid to avenge her. Had she lived, she was ruined. She was *prastlo,* dishonored. No Roma man would've wanted her."

"This girl was an innocent and the law would've sided with the Gypsies," Amelia said. "I cannot believe your tale."

"Believe it." Luca bent to dab the wetness from his knee. Infection oozed through his double pair of hose and breeches. Idly, he fingered the spots of blood. "He's the same man who wants Lady Blakwell to live with him in London. Be assured I'll not permit him to take her."

"There's nothing you can do." Amelia fixed her stare on his knee. "My lady has shut herself in the dining room with endless cups of tea and feigned illness until Lord Crispin departs."

Deadly somber, Luca focused on the dining room door. "I'll seek Patience on my own."

How easy it was, he thought grimly, to call the countess by her given name and break English society's damn, strict rules.

Amelia caught his arm. "Don't. You'll get us all killed."

He shook off her hand and grabbed his walking stick. "Keep watch and alert me when Crispin returns."

"I don't answer to you, Mr. Gypsy."

A thread of lively Roma curses came to his lips. He shared them freely with Amelia, then bound across the room. Two steps at a time, his boots resonated like abrupt drum taps on the floor. When he reached the dining room door, he stopped short and let his breathing slow.

He entered without a sound, latched the door closed, and set his pouch on a side chair. The dining room greeting him was not as luxurious as he expected. A pewter pitcher was set on the buffet table, along with a silver tea service, some spoons, sugar and cream. Angled in a wingback chair close to the fireplace, an array of rainbow colored thread lay scattered atop a sewing basket.

Oliver slept near the hooded fireplace. Except for a subtle twitch of his tail, the dog hardly moved. Too late, it occurred to Luca that he should've knocked first. His conscience nagged that Patience wouldn't welcome his interruption. He ordered his conscience to stay silent.

Her back to him, she gazed outdoors at the rain beginning to stream against the paned glass. Lacking the energy she normally displayed, she toyed with the silken curtain sash. Her hands were small and graceful, her movements refined.

Without turning, Patience asked, "Was Crispin shouting in the drawing room because he played the wrong chord at the end of the Sonata again, Amelia?"

Luca willed his legs forward. He willed his hands to reach out and give her shoulders a supportive squeeze. He did neither. What he did made the least bit of sense because it was so contrary to his impetuous nature.

He placed his walking stick on the floor. Then he did nothing. Absolutely nothing. He merely stayed where he was and stared at her like a besotted swain.

She'd shed her confining mob cap. Her hair shimmered to a rich red-gold in the wavering afternoon sun. She'd secured her mass of curls at the top of her crown with an assortment of pins. A curvy strand tumbled across her cheek and prevented him from seeing her face, only the tilt of her small, turned-up nose. A delicate vision, she seemed too light and airy to be real.

"Amelia?" Patience repeated. "I pray that Crispin will find a tavern in town and never return. He can't force me to live with him in London, can he?" Her posture was rigid.

"Nay, he can't," Luca said.

Patience dropped the sash and swiveled.

Luca's admiring gaze wandered to her shoulders and the exposed, freckled skin of her neckline. His pulse kicked, pounding through his legs, up his stomach and chest, settling at the base of his throat. When he spoke again, his voice grew husky with an uncharted emotion he couldn't name. "You're looking as lovely as ever on this bleak day, *kamadiyo*."

Her eyes rounded. A war of confusion and relief seemed to battle across her expressive face. She laced her hands together and clasped them to her heart.

"Mr. Boldor. I ... I waited so long. I wasn't sure if I'd ever see you again."

"A misunderstanding I wanted to correct as soon as I was able."

She accompanied the nervous edge of her laugh with a jaunty shake of her head. "You almost made me swoon."

"A brave woman like you never swoons."

"I swooned only once in my life, when I feared you'd fallen to your death."

A smile dawned as he gazed at her exquisite face. "Surely a grand leap out another window might grant me another swoon?" His gaze roamed to her frock. Auburn suited her. Auburn was the color of her hair by firelight and complemented the creaminess of her complexion.

Her hands flew to her neckline as a sheen of color washed her temples. "Why are you here?"

"It seems the question on everyone's tongue this afternoon," he said.

She tilted her head, waiting for an answer he couldn't say aloud.

Because I missed you so very, very much and couldn't stay away a moment longer.

The words had come into his mind without warning. He glanced about the dining room to be certain he hadn't spoken them. He'd never missed anyone in his life. Hell, he'd never cared about anyone enough to miss them. Missing someone spoke of commitment. Certainly, he'd never utter such phrases to a highborn English lady.

He kneaded the taut muscles at the back of his neck. "I came back in case you needed protection from some terrible men. And it seems as though your stepson is one of them."

Tears welled in her eyes. She licked her lips and splayed her hands across her chest. "What am I going to do?" she whispered. Her voice choked with tears. "I can't live with Crispin in London. I can't."

"I can assure you that you won't."

"He's charging me with his father's murder and there's no way to prove my innocence." The color rose in her cheeks. "And if we go to court, he'll win...I know he'll win, the solicitor had said as much when I'd met with him...but I was hoping... And I'll be thrown in prison for a crime I didn't commit if I don't agree to abide by Crispin's demands." Her gaze darted to the doorway. She shivered and rubbed her arms, rocking back and forth.

Luca grabbed her shoulders. "He won't win. I won't let him win. I'll fight anyone who'd ever try to hurt you."

Brave words, although inside, Luca felt helpless. He could no longer demand that she live with him in his tribe, for she'd be hunted by the law. Her life, their lives together, were at the mercy of her vile stepson.

He looked to the floor, uncomfortable, harboring foolish fantasies pointing to a life they were never destined to lead.

His chest tightened while he planned, obsessed, about what to do next.

"I can take care of myself." Patience pulled away. Clearly, she was thinking the same thing he was. Her hand twirled the wisp of hair along her neck and he watched her innocent, modest motions. She was no innocent, he corrected himself. She'd been married several years. Jealousy unexpectedly knocked and Luca clamped his fists together to sheath the eruption of possessiveness at the thought of her living with her stepson.

Nay. That would never happen.

CHAPTER TWENTY-THREE

*L*uca's dark, strong form had come upon Patience with unspoken confidence. Glossy, black hair flowed around his face, his orange scarf tied to one side of his forehead.

He'd come back.

Impulsively, she lifted her fingers to smooth a gleaming lock from his temple. He grabbed her wrists and looped her hands around his nape.

"I'm so grateful and relieved that you've returned. I can't believe you're here, or that you're real," she said.

He switched his weight to his other leg. His face reflected a pain he didn't bother to hide. "Be assured, I'm very real."

She glided her fingertips over the prickle of his beard, then found the corded muscles in his shoulders, kneading the tightness. His body was like him—gruff and tender—a man of startling contrasts. She couldn't stop touching him. So peculiar, for she was a woman who flinched whenever a man tried to pierce her invisible armor by a chance touch of his hand.

"I watched the fields and worried for your safety," she said. "Sometimes I thought I saw you walking along one of the paths, although I was always mistaken. If you were here, you'd keep yourself hidden." She conceded a disparaging smile at her habit of blurting out whatever was on her mind. However, there was little point in trying to hide her joy at seeing him again, her relief at having him near.

Because she was a friend worried about a friend, her reasonable brain prompted. Certainly a strong Gypsy man could take care of himself. However, her heart disagreed with her logic, her happiness too genuine. He had returned. He had returned. He had returned.

Tears formed behind her eyes and worked down her throat.

"I wondered if you ever thought about me all the while you were with your tribe," she added.

He stayed quiet, neither moving nor taking a breath. Apparently, he was impervious to the fact this was the part where he should loudly declare that he'd thought of her as often as she'd thought of him. After all, *he'd* come back to *her*.

He turned his head and pinned his gaze not on her face, nor on her person.

He rested his gaze on the dining room chair. The setting afternoon sun weaved a patchwork of rich orange and pink shades on the silk curtains.

"Be assured I won't leave again, especially since Crispin is here," Luca said, instead of answering her question. "Although he's young, Pulko is managing. However, I'll need to look in on my tribe frequently." Luca's smile wavered, two conflicts playing on his features.

His fingers began a leisurely ascent up her spine.

She studied him for several beats longer than she should have and an ache filled her rash heart. She turned, moved away from him, and looked out the window at the river beyond the fields.

Luca came to stand behind her. This was them together,

contented and peaceful. The realization lifted her heart and placed it gently back in her chest.

The last splatter of daylight spilled through the arched glass and she drew the silken curtain sash closed, then turned to him. Only the dwindling embers in the fireplace lit the dining room. She swung toward the mantel to light some candles.

His body blocked hers, although he didn't raise his arms. "I'm happy to be here," he said softly, forcing her to stand with her back against the window frame, facing him. "I made the right decision in returning to you."

Her heart soared a little too perilously. He was hard to resist, especially to a woman who hadn't experienced the headiness of desire in a long time. To bring herself back to earth, she tried to keep in mind who she was, where she was, and that she'd vowed never to trust a man again. How long would he stay this time? Had he really returned for good?

"Why is someone like you so interested in visiting and protecting someone like me? 'Tis because I'm a noblewoman and you want to enjoy the luxuries of English living?"

"You state the reasons that make me want to turn away." Luca grinned, dipped his head, and caught her lips with his. The kiss was over before it began, his warm breath glancing her cheeks. She stayed where she was, rooted to the floor, the cold glass of the windowpane pressing against her back.

He took her hands and tucked them in his grasp. "Do you trust that I'll keep you safe?"

"Aye," she said.

Believing, trusting, safety...For a Gypsy rogue, he was so concerned about honest and just principles, yet he relied on no one, had faith in no one, depended on no one.

The dull sound of a cold rain dashed against the window.

His thumb pad brushed against her palm like rough-hewn

wood. "I'm not your elderly husband. I'll never hurt you." Luca brushed a kiss along her cheekbone, then stared at her and grinned roguishly. "I'm a Romany man with few learned skills, although I've been told that I have a decided skill for kissing, especially for a beautiful woman I've missed very much."

This was precisely how he went about enchanting her.

She stepped away. "My stepson's due to return shortly."

"As a favor to me, Amelia is keeping watch for his return and will notify us with ample warning."

Patience's lips moved in a silent question. Before she could ask why Amelia agreed to such a favor, Luca gave an amused shrug of his shoulders. "I eavesdropped on her entire conversation with your stepson. Your cat and I found a splendid spot in the pantry."

"You seem to be on affable terms with Amelia."

"She's a splendid ally." Luca extended his arm in a gracious gesture and stood to the side. "Of course, if you wish to leave now, you certainly can."

So she was free to leave. Free to rally right past him out of her own dining room and into her own kitchen. She glided around him so they stood a few feet apart.

"I don't know how we'll resolve this situation, although I promise you'll be safe," he added.

It wasn't Luca's promise that kept her hands at her sides. It was his self-assurance keeping her feet firmly planted on the floor.

She shook her head. "You don't understand. My stepson is a madman, a description far too generous if he found us together."

"I'll help you figure out a way to get the best of your stepson."

She blew a strand of hair off her forehead. "Perhaps Gypsy

men prefer triple jeopardy, and are attracted to women possessing a cloud of auburn hair and freckles on their face."

"I'm merely a man who returned to the woman who afforded me protection, to now extend my own."

CHAPTER TWENTY-FOUR

*P*atience glanced at the window, noting the darkening shadows. "The servants and my stepson should've returned by now."

"Crispin's in the village, no doubt deep in his cups."

An insistent rap on the dining room door, followed by Amelia's insistent whisper, interrupted them.

"Lady Blakwell, your stepson is walking up the road from the stables. Is Mr. Gypsy there?"

"I'll answer for both of us." Luca reached into his boot and yanked a silver dagger from its sheath.

Patience blinked at his startling transformation. He no longer resembled the man who'd kissed her gently a few scant minutes ago, nor the man who'd suffered a horrific gouge on his leg and closed his eyes to shut out the pain.

He steadied one hand on the side of the chair. In four measured strides he reached the door and pressed his body against it. Slowly, he raised the dagger. "Is anyone with you, Amelia?"

"I'm alone," Amelia answered, "Although there'll be

servants milling about soon, especially if the countess doesn't make an appearance in the kitchen."

Luca sheathed the dagger and placed it back into his boot.

"Your stepson should enter the hallway shortly," Amelia said. "I'll deter him. However, he'll become suspicious if I stall too long. And, he mentioned that he'd invited a guest for dinner."

When Amelia's footsteps receded, Luca stayed by the door, grim and silent.

He could've been doing any number of things—retrieving his pouch, buffing his boots, grabbing his tan cloak to depart. He did nothing of the sort. Instead, he occupied himself with simple tasks that normally took seconds—securing his green sash, readjusting his linen shirt, retying the tattered hose around his leg.

She lifted an eyebrow and stared at him. "If Crispin catches you, he'll kill you and ruin my life in the bargain. Depart now, and remain unseen."

Luca trudged to the window. She noted that his footsteps were heavy and his injured leg dragged. He lifted the curtains and peered at the darkening fields. The little snow left shimmered by the light of an early moon, the window fogging with the heat of his warm breath.

She squeezed her eyes shut, trying to accept what was best for them both. He needed to leave, for his safety as well as her own. He had a tribe to take care of, she had a murder charge to fight while enduring the caresses of her depraved stepson.

She pressed her lips together, reminding herself that a lady must accept whatever life brought her with dignity and grace. With that thought, her spine straightened. Yet her heart shied from the realization, the reality, that a woman and a Gypsy man couldn't fight a London judge and jury.

She gazed at him. She tried to memorize the bump on his nose, his soothing, easy smile.

"Goodbye, Mr. Boldor," she said. "Please be safe."

"I'm not going anywhere."

She glanced at the door. "If you wait much longer, you'll be trapped. You can't tramp past my stepson as he comes into the front hallway."

"'Twould appear that danger lurks in every corner and I'm the only Gypsy knight available."

She shook her head. He spouted cool male bravery, whereas she turned into a stammering fool who tripped over her own tongue.

"My stepson will pull you apart limb by limb if he discovers you here," she said.

"I'm not afraid, Patience."

She blinked. "First you become familiar with my name and now you believe you can fight a murder conviction with no money nor power? What's your grievance with my stepson, anyway? You don't know him like I do."

Luca clenched his fists. "I know him better. He brutally raped and murdered a Roma girl I once knew and left her dead by a raging river."

Patience stiffened and couldn't respond. She only knew that she had to be near Luca because she needed his comforting presence. She stepped to the window beside him. The early evening seemed solemn, the sky growing as sad as his words. She scoured her temples, hard, to take away the images he described.

"Each time I see you, you create more and more havoc in my life," she said.

"Each time I see you, you create more and more meaning in mine." His voice came perfectly soft. He was forever bent on captivating, his magnetism weaving an illusion of happily ever after.

She shook her head. "After all these months, are you now attempting to court me?"

"Is that what you English call it? Then, the answer is 'aye.'" He smiled, all coolness and charisma. "I'll go up to the attic and stay out of sight. You count slowly for two minutes, then go directly into the kitchen to supervise dinner preparations."

He'd reverted to his favorite authoritative tone, the one that made her itch to defy him.

"You cannot command me to count, go, and supervise," she said. "There are more ways of solving problems than assuming you're the new lord of my manor and can dictate all that will happen."

"I'll never be the lord of any English manor." A flicker flashed through his eyes, then his face went expressionless. "I'll meet you in the drawing room at midnight so we can formulate a plan. The servants will be safely asleep by then. In the meantime, I'll listen in on your dinner with Crispin for ideas on how to get you free of his charges. I promise I'll stay hidden."

She flung her hands to her hips. "'Tis too dangerous."

Rapid footsteps sounding from the hallway diverted them. "Lord Crispin is coming," Amelia called through the door.

"Midnight," Luca promised. With the prowess of a sleek panther, he swung the dining room door open, then closed the door behind him.

CHAPTER TWENTY-FIVE

a quarter of an hour, Patience decided, was ample time to dress for dinner, especially when she had no interest in impressing her stepson with her appearance.

Since their confrontation when he'd first arrived and played the pianoforte, she'd managed to avoid Crispin. His flinty stare terrified her. When they'd passed on the path to the stables, or by the kitchen pantry, the hairs on the back of her neck rose and her breath came jerky. In the torchlight, she felt his eyes appraise her as a prized lamb before the slaughter. She'd clutched the swansdown of her woolen pelisse firmly to her neckline, confronted his bravado with a blue-blooded look of disdain, then hastened her steps to get away from him.

After looking in on Cook and the kitchen servants, Patience climbed the stairs and latched her bedchamber door. She bathed at her washbasin and walked to her closet to rummage through her wardrobe. With Amelia's assistance, she chose a short-sleeved black frock trimmed at the waist with white satin ribbons. Amelia snapped a brush through

Patience's hair and confined her unmanageable curls to the crown.

After Amelia left the bedchamber, Patience regarded herself in the mirror. Auburn ringlets framed her cheeks, and her youthful face smiled back at her. Marriage had done unspeakable things to her body, but hadn't changed her clear, trusting expression.

She secured a black, sheer mob cap over her head and proceeded to the hallway.

Poised on the top of the stairwell, she pulled on a pair of long white gloves.

Midnight. She was meeting Luca at midnight, here, in her own house. Although she'd spent many hours with him, the thought made her color rise.

As she rounded the last step on the stairwell, she spotted Digby laying out the blue and white tableware and gleaming silver pieces on the dining room table. The clinking of porcelain echoed through the hall. Shiny copper plates filled with nuts and pyramids of sweetmeat set grandly on the side tables.

Her stepson milled by the fireplace. He wore a green cravat at his throat tied with a large bow, and showed off his foppishness in an absurdly tight-fitting waistcoat and matching breeches of the finest blue velvet.

Patience made her way to the kitchen to supervise last-minute preparations. The clashing odors of fennel and mint greeted her. She gagged and caught hold of the doorway as her legs swayed.

"Are you feeling unwell, my lady?" Amelia asked from the kitchen. "Your face is ashen."

With a shaky hand, Patience wiped a line of sweat pooling beneath her mob cap. "The smell of fennel has never agreed with me."

"Since you were a child, mackerel sprinkled with fennel

seed has always been one of your favorite dishes," Amelia affirmed.

Patience swallowed the sickness in her throat and held onto the doorway. "I cannot explain my stomach of late. The simplest odor sets my insides roiling, although the nausea will pass."

Amelia picked up a knife and moved to the chopping table.

"What dessert is planned?" Patience asked. "I've noticed that the kitchen pantry is desperately low on spices and sweeteners."

"Ice cream, although it's quite melted," Amelia said with sham repentance.

Before Patience could remark on serving melted ice cream, Amelia bent to Patience's ear and whispered, "Has Mr. Gypsy gone back to his tribe?"

"He's upstairs in the attic, and said that he'll be staying, although one never knows for certain with him," Patience whispered back. "I'm supposed to see him at midnight."

Amelia's lips widened into the closest beam of endorsement she'd ever displayed. "Wonderful."

"You truly believe 'tis a wonderful idea for a Gypsy to meet me in the drawing room at midnight, with Crispin so near? 'Tis too perilous," Patience whispered.

Amelia grabbed Patience's arm and steered her to a far corner of the room. "Not for him," Amelia whispered. "You won't be in any danger. Mr. Gypsy is the finest, bravest man I've ever met, and he's captivated with you. I approve."

Patience held her gasp. If Amelia had called Luca the most refined man on earth, she wouldn't have been more astonished. Besides chiding Patience to conduct herself as a proper Christian lady, Amelia found fault with every man, declaring the lot of them selfish rascals. Why, Amelia had devoted the greater part of her life, up until Patience married, keeping Patience apart from men. Especially after Patience's adolescent tryst with her smooth-talking cousin.

She sighed. Well, she'd paid dearly for her one night of imprudence with a malicious scar, followed by a resulting scandal and unending humiliation, resulting in the ultimate sacrifice, her marriage to a cruel man.

"You no longer think of Mr. Boldor as a barbarian?" Patience whispered.

"Sometimes, when he has that untamed, faraway look in his eye." With that disheartening comment, Amelia waddled to the stove on the far end of the kitchen to commend Cook for burning the mutton, then laid claim to a stool at the kitchen table.

Patience shook her head, deciding to leave the kitchen preparations to Amelia. She left the kitchen, fastened a cordial smile to her face, and entered the drawing room.

~

"Good evening, my lady," Digby said, not because he had any interest in her, merely out of duty. He narrowed his stance, his features void of any interest but politeness. He handed her a cup of green tea which Patience hoped would settle her unending nausea.

Crispin sat on a wingback chair near the fireplace. "Lady Blakwell, how pleasant to have your company at dinner. You haven't joined me for any meals since I arrived."

She shuddered at the eeriness of presiding over a dinner with her stepson.

"I wouldn't have missed our final meal together." She cringed as she spoke.

"'Tis temporary. Soon we'll be together, after final preparations in London are made." Crispin twisted partly in the wingback chair, then slowly rose to his feet. "Amelia will be dismissed when you move in with me. She's growing too old to travel."

Instinctively, Patience jerked back as he strode toward her. "Amelia is accustomed to the hard work involved in keeping our estate self-sustaining. I plan to continue to reside in Ipswich with her."

Crispin narrowed his eyes. "Unfortunately, her uncle needs her in Bucklesham."

Patience bit back her response. Crispin knew her attachment to her maid and the obvious unfairness of letting go a servant who'd devoted her life to Patience and her family. Resolutely, she took a sip of tea and allowed the pleasurable sweetness of milk and sugar to ease her throat and quiet her stomach.

"I met someone in the village yesterday," Crispin resumed.

Patience poised her teacup at her lips. "Who?"

"My father's old acquaintance, the Most Honorable Christopher Haringley, Marquess of Wottingham. He favored me by accepting my invitation to dine with us this evening."

Unable to see the marquess, Patience stepped closer to the dining room and placed her cup on an end table. Extending her hand, she smiled at the handsome older man grinning at her.

"Lord Haringley," she said.

Placing his shaking grip on the chair's side arms, the marquess stood, removed his gloves, and held out his hand. Obligingly, she placed her right hand in his and gave a slight curtsey.

"Lady Blakwell." He brushed his lips over her gloved knuckles. "Such a pleasure to see you again."

"Your presence this evening is a great gift," she answered sincerely.

He was taller than she recalled, with a slim build and alert brown eyes studying her in speculative detail. His white cravat and linen shirt were immaculate beneath a double breasted indigo waistcoat. His hair was graying but showed signs of once being jet-black. Something about him seemed faintly recognizable and definitely disturbing.

"May I extend my belated condolences on the death of your husband, the Earl of Ipswich," the marquess said. "My business has taken me abroad these last few years, and I carved out time when I returned to visit my son, Edmund, in Wiltshire. One never knows what mischief he's been up to. Then I arrived in Ipswich less than a fortnight ago. How fortunate I met up with your stepson in the village."

"How fortunate, indeed," she murmured.

"I mentioned to the marquess that our dinner this evening is more or less a celebration," Crispin said, snapping her awareness back to him. "Do we have cause to celebrate?"

She gave her ringlets a proud toss. "We can certainly celebrate your return to London."

Crispin raised his glass of Ratafia, a sweet cordial, and gestured to the marquess. "My lovely stepmother is considering my proposal to move to London with me. This estate is too large for a widow to manage by herself and I fear for her safety."

"My decisions are slow," she said, wanting to add that he'd left her no choice, but saying nothing. Avoiding Crispin's scowl, she looked at the marquess. His dark eyes lit with warmth and understanding.

"Apparently your stepmother needs more time to come to a decision, Lord Crispin," the marquess said. "Women cannot be pushed into something unless they're convinced 'tis what they want. Otherwise, all the prodding in the world does little good."

Crispin fingered his cravat and glanced at the clock. "Six fifteen. I distinctly recall telling the maid to serve our meal promptly at six."

As if prompted by his statement, the servants marched into the dining room with great ceremony. Two maids in black wearing white ruffled aprons balanced trays filled with hot artichoke soup, pickled vegetables, and baked mackerel. They seemed coolly unconcerned with the burnt mutton they placed in the center of the dining room table.

After she and her guests took their seats around the dining room table, Patience asked for a moment of prayer before they ate. When they finished their prayer, Crispin tasted the soup and his conversing froze. Meanwhile, the marquess stabbed at the seared fat bubbling atop the mutton.

From across the dining room, Patience read Amelia's beam of satisfaction. She'd deliberately prepared the worst meal in Ipswich's history, a mutinous and dangerous attempt to antagonize Crispin.

Half-listening to the conversation swirling around her, Patience felt a smidge of guilt. She should've realized what Amelia had been up to. The marquess was an older man and her guest, and deserved a prompt and decent meal. With a sigh, she fixed her stare on a cobweb in the corner of the ceiling and tried to determine how long it had been there.

&

*D*inner pushed on. Glasses and cups were lowered and lifted. For two hours, food was eaten in a combination of slow motion and a blur. Except for the plink of silver and the charming exploits of the marquess's journeys abroad, the meal consisted of a silent downhill slide of inedible food culminating in dessert.

When the hour neared nine o'clock and the men were about to retire to the drawing room to enjoy their port, Patience turned to the marquess. "You're welcome to stay the night. We have several spare bedchambers available in the other wing of the house, where Lord Crispin stays."

"Your consideration is appreciated, but an old man enjoys his own comfortable surroundings." With a kindly nod he pushed back his chair and stood, thanked them for the meal, then called for his servant to send his carriage round.

After the marquess departed, she bid Crispin a hastened good night.

He watched her. She knew he did, felt his interest boring into her back, as a cat awaiting a wingless wren. And she also knew if she were not extremely vigilant and didn't have Luca by her side, she would never be safe from any man named Blakwell.

CHAPTER TWENTY-SIX

*F*rom childhood, Patience had been taught that the stroke of midnight was a time to dread. A bewitching hour. A time for elusive phantoms.

She knew better now. She believed in God.

With an assurance from Amelia that Patience's dog, Oliver, was content to sleep in the kitchen, Patience entered her bedchamber well before midnight.

Then she waited. And waited.

And waited, before slipping quietly down the stairs to sit on the settee in the drawing room.

The first hour went by with no sign of a Gypsy man with soft black eyes. She stared out the window, fidgeted with the sash, and counted the ragged clouds floating across a hazy evening sky. Slowly, the second hour ticked by.

Patience scolded herself for allowing disappointed tears to press against her throat. If anything, she should shout for joy. He gave her emotions a reprieve, for he wasn't coming.

In her own house. In her own drawing room. He wasn't coming.

To her chagrin, the tears reached her eyes. She blinked

them away, unpinned her ringlets, then cast her black mob cap on the walnut table near the pianoforte. It mattered naught if he'd fallen asleep and forgotten. She wouldn't be going up to the attic to find him.

The heartless scoundrel.

When the third hour straggled with no sign of him, she resigned herself to the fact that she was, once again, a fool in putting her trust in a man. A fool who thought a man might actually care about her, and not want something in repayment —a dowry, land, or more of herself than she could give. A fool who'd fallen for a charismatic Gypsy's honeyed ways and endless charms and false promises. A fool who'd succumbed to the hope that Luca embodied all a man was supposed to be. Honest. Sincere. Heroic. With an inner sigh of regret, she reminded herself that there was no such man.

Woodenly, she crept up the stairs and prepared for bed. She scrubbed herself with lavender bar soap and donned clean linen night clothes. She yawned, so tired her eyelids leaked.

The logs shifted, the flames sparked and grew dim. She shuffled to the fireplace and warmed her hands. Then she locked her door. Twice. And crept into bed.

～

*S*he always could tell when someone was watching her, even in sleep. She kept her eyes closed, knowing someone stood over her bed. It was not unlikely, nor unusual. Her late husband had entered her bedchamber whenever he pleased.

Caught between dreams and wakefulness, she inhaled, expecting the reek of vinegary herbs. Not a man who smelled of outdoor campfires and warm leather and worn buckskin.

She jolted up.

Lit by twin candles on her night table, Luca's wildly hand-some face hovered over her. "Did you sleep well, *kamadiyo*?" His warm breath skimmed over her cheeks.

She gazed into his dark eyes and shoved off the blankets. Scrambling to her feet, she grabbed her shawl hanging by the doorway.

He was all handsomeness, all attraction, all too real.

"How long did you watch me?" she managed to ask, scurrying into the hallway barefoot.

He followed her. The top laces of his linen shirt were loosened, his green sash tied at his waist. "I came as promised."

"You're late."

Something flashed in his eyes. Surprise? Interest? Both quickly masked.

"I'm sorry. You waited up for me?" he asked.

She hesitated. The hint of hopefulness in his tone disarmed her. "I waited in the drawing room as you'd requested."

"My tribe had an urgent matter requiring my attention," he said. "I solved the matter without having to travel far, thanks to Pulko."

His tribe came first and she could ask for nothing more than his steadfast caring for them. Still, she felt rebellious. "You were able to walk to the tribe's encampment and back in one night?"

He gave his typically cool smile. "I told you, I didn't need to travel far."

She directed her gaze to the small hallway window and stared out at the stars, sparkling like diamonds against a black sky. "Crispin's sleeping in the other wing in one of the guest bedchambers. Being with you here is too risky."

"He's *beng*, evil, and you cannot be in this dower house alone with him. I'd contemplated making a *bender* at the edge of your estate and sleeping there until he departed. And then I decided to sleep in the attic as you requested because 'tis closer to you."

She tossed her hands on her hips. "You'd *decided* to sleep in the attic? You overbearing—"

"Gypsy rogue," he finished with a smile.

She allowed herself a moment of frosty silence to stare icily at him while caution clamored in her ears. This was precisely how he went about luring her back into believing he truly cared about her.

"Remember you asked if I wanted to court you?" he asked.

"What an unusual way to go about it—by sneaking into my bedchamber in the middle of the night and scaring me half to death. Shall I add you were also late while my immoral stepson sleeps under my roof?"

He glanced his knuckles over her cheeks. "Trust me. I came back to protect you."

Her respect for him multiplied by his ability to speak openly. He exposed her apprehension for what it was—a nameless panic. The longer she knew him, the more she enjoyed his companionship and the sometimes playful, sometimes serious, sparring they shared. For these simple delights, and the happiness filling her whenever he stepped within ten feet of her, she was willing to believe that she could trust him. He made her chuckle out loud with an impudent remark, his white teeth flashing in his sun-burnished face as he laughed with her. Or, he made her flush with elation when he told her how lovely she looked.

He swept out his hands in an invitation. "Are you ready to go back to sleep? In less than a few hours it will be dawn."

With a shake of her head, she stepped to her bedchamber door. "Truly you're the most impossible man to understand," she said.

"Enigmatic sounds better."

Enigmatic. She added a few words of her own. Mysterious, resourceful, and possessing a wonderful, wry intelligence she never would've anticipated when she'd first met him.

"The truth is, I'm relieved, yet frightened that you're here," she admitted.

He pushed the persistent ringlets from her forehead. "I'll never hurt you."

"I'm not frightened of you," she said. "I'm frightened of myself."

"Sometimes I'm frightened of myself, also." He brushed his lips against her temple. "And know that 'tis a terrible strain on my arms not to keep you in them."

He must've realized his candid confession would soften her limbs to butter. She felt split in two, as if she watched a woman she thought she knew from across the length of the dark hallway. Clutching her shawl closer, she padded across the threshold of her bedchamber and stood close to the doorway.

He kept his gaze on her face and gave her hands a gentle squeeze. "My beautiful countess, I cannot think clearly when we're so close and what I need to say cannot be casually spoken." He spoke low, as if he pondered some serious conversation he'd been having with himself, thoroughly weighed the consequences, and didn't like the outcome. She hoped for the mischievous twinkle to reappear in his eyes, the rough angles of his face to ease, his calm tone to reassure her that all was fine.

He stepped back, keeping a few feet from her. Whatever he had to say was important, and the inkling of apprehension welled in her chest. She tried to quell her uneasiness and turned to glance out the window at the desolate, leafless trees in the distance. The bright yellow moon had started its descent in the last hours before dawn.

"I watched you tonight, wrapped in your fine shawl," Luca

began. "And I realized how accustomed you are to elegance. Have you ever slept outdoors in a tent?"

"Nay."

"Have you ever eaten a meal cooked over a campfire?"

"Never."

"I like to sleep under the stars," he said. "I like to watch the waves storming the coast during a thunderstorm, build a campfire in a circle of grass, skin and cook a rabbit I hunted."

"These are the qualities I admire most about you," she said, cautiously trying to gauge his mood. "Your culture, your beliefs, your closeness to nature. You're a man of principle."

"You admire the Romany in me, the best part. But what you're not aware of—" He leaned heavily against the wall, a few steps from her, like a man planning to push through an uncomfortable conversation that he'd initiated.

"What?" she asked.

He walked past her into her bedchamber, led her further into the room, and latched the door behind them. He reached for his waistcoat, which he'd placed on a high wardrobe near the door. His worn cloak followed. He yanked the orange scarf from the seam of his cloak. "Do you know where I was this evening?"

"Tending to your tribe," she ventured.

"Before that. While you enjoyed dinner in the dining room, I assisted Amelia in the kitchen burning the mutton to a crisp when the other servants left the room. Then I hid and listened in on the dinner conversations."

Disconcerted because he was actually talking about food, about burnt mutton and dinner conversations, Patience could only blink.

"I watched your stepson. And I watched your guest, also," Luca said slowly.

"Are you referring to the marquess? He's an elderly, long-time acquaintance and a very kind man."

Luca's eyes sparked, then went flat. So subtle, but she'd seen it.

"He's not kind."

"You know him?" she asked.

She thought Luca flinched, but couldn't be sure.

The tenseness in his body seemed to weigh down the air, making it too heavy to catch her breath. Although he didn't move, she felt him withdrawing, farther and farther away. Soon he'd be only a shadow of a person she once knew, forever out of reach.

"Aye," Luca replied evenly.

"He's generous to his servants. He travels abroad a great deal and recently returned to Ipswich."

A contemptuous snicker pinched Luca's lips. "I know."

"You don't seem to be the type of man to—"

"To grace the same social circles as an English countess, or the esteemed noble peerage?"

"I'm uncomfortable in these circles, as well." There, she'd admitted her lack of confidence, her shrinking into herself whenever she was confronted by a group of wealthy nobility. She knew people whispered and laughed at her scarred face behind their polite, blank facades.

"So how are you acquainted with the marquess?" she persisted.

Luca seemed so uneasy, so defensive, unwilling to allow her into his dark, secretive world.

Two more steps brought him to her bedchamber door. He fumbled with the latch. "He's the part of me I loathe, the proper English part. Lord Christopher Haringley, Marquess of Wottingham, is my despicable father."

CHAPTER TWENTY-SEVEN

"*Y*our father?"

Luca had expected the shock in her voice, the confusion on her face.

But not the suspicion. Not the anger.

Patience pushed past him and shored her back against the bedchamber door. "You never told me you were of noble blood." Her manner accused, shaking with skepticism and disbelief.

"You never asked."

She threw furious daggers with her eyes, sharp as switchblades. "So you decided 'twas best to deceive me? Recuperate in my attic for a sennight, sneak into my bedchamber for an evening—cover me with primrose words—but exclude the fact that you're the son of an English noble?" She shook her head furiously. "You lied by omission. I believed you, tended to you, thought you trustworthy."

"I am."

As he watched her distrustful expression, a wretched feeling hollowed out a place in his stomach. He wanted her confidence and admired her unswerving faith in God, yet

Luca had betrayed her by omission. Her God was judgmental. Her God wouldn't be pleased.

"You assumed I was a Roma beggar because of my dark skin. Perhaps you have a misguided sense of what people should look like, what place they should hold in your ideal, pure English world."

She balked, shrinking into the door, as if she didn't believe he was sincere, as if he'd changed into a mythical dragon from a folklore where she didn't belong.

"It doesn't matter to me if you're the lowliest vagrant in England."

He reached out to touch her hand. "I returned to protect you, but also because I missed you very much. You were constantly in my thoughts."

The pink blush on her cheeks rose to her temples. Her shining blue eyes searched his face. "I'm not inexperienced to your attempts to reel me into your net with insincere words."

"Because I'm a Gypsy and therefore beneath a noblewoman like you?" he countered.

"Because you're a scoundrel who preys on my benevolence."

He stiffened. She'd meant to hurt him. And she had. "Alms for the poor?" he drawled bitterly. "You're most charitable, my lady, to help someone less fortunate."

"Can you ever get over this hatred of your father, and by all extension, all English?" she asked.

He blinked. Perhaps he'd been naive in thinking they could figure out a way to be together happily and build a life together. He watched her expression, saw the quiet look of desperation in her eyes. Perhaps she was having the same doubts.

Patience whirled and opened her bedchamber door. "Go."

He gazed at her. She looked extraordinarily gorgeous in that ivory linen nightdress, framed by a sweep of reddish-gold hair, her cheekbones enhanced by a crimson wash of fury.

"I'm no pitiable scoundrel," he said. "And you should know enough about the Roma by now to realize that we don't take lightly to insults."

She stood tall for a small woman, rocking on her tiptoes. "My insults have only begun. Grab your feather quill and scroll for the long list ahead."

The charged silence lasted several minutes before she finally spoke again.

"This has been a difficult and trying few fortnights." Her breath was tight, but her eyes softened. "I didn't mean my earlier remarks. They came out all wrong and I'm sorry."

He nodded. "Apology accepted."

"You didn't need my charity, although surely you needed food and a warm room when you were suffering so."

He pulled off his orange scarf. It dropped to the floor. "Never, ever pity me."

"I have no reason to pity an English nobleman. 'Tis more likely I'd pity a Gypsy beggar."

"What about a half-breed?" His words slipped out, demanding. Meaningful.

He averted his eyes to escape her answer, for it was better left unsaid.

"Why is your heritage of such importance?" she asked.

He motioned to her bedchamber. "'Tis of utmost importance to a well-bred aristocrat, is it not? Blood lines and good breeding are the main topics of conversation in a proper English drawing room."

She replied without hesitation. "You're fortunate to belong to two races and two cultures. You reap the benefits of each."

"Perhaps I belong to neither." He kept his expression nonchalant, but the troubling reality of his mixed heritage almost broke him as a child, as a young man, as an adult. He was forever obsessed with being the bravest, the strongest, the most agile, all to prove his self-worth.

"Do you prefer an Englishman or a Rom?" he asked.

She bent to pick up his orange scarf and handed it to him. "You're exactly as you should be."

"My Englishness is a millstone around my neck," he said. "The Romanes elders still regard me with suspicion if I do anything they don't approve of."

A torrent of emotions flew across Patience's face before settling into shining eyes and a kind smile. "You took on an oppressive burden caring for an impoverished Gypsy tribe and have never shirked your responsibilities. The elders should be grateful."

Just thinking about the endless hunger and countless deprivations of his tribe filled Luca's chest with commitment and duty. He strode into her bedchamber and to the window, opened it part way, and shoved the silk draperies wide. He gulped a chilly breath. All was serene and silent. Not even a breeze glanced the hedges and hazelnut trees.

"The Rom are good to me," he said softly. "My tribe could've rejected my mother. She'd taken up with a *gadje*, a serious offense for a Roma. They accepted her pregnancy by an Englishman, they accepted me, a half-breed, even after her death."

There was more, but he couldn't speak of it. The twin baby brother who'd died, his mother's sorrow and despair. The long winter days broken only by her muffled crying.

This was his life. Always a struggle. Always such sadness. He gripped the window frame and closed his eyes, concentrating on the darkness to blot the memories.

Patience came to stand by him and rested her hand on his forearm. "Pray for guidance and listen for a quiet, inner voice."

He shook his head. Pray. He honestly didn't know how.

"When did you last see your father besides this evening?" she asked.

Luca opened his eyes and stared out the window. "I saw him a few times over the years. We've never spoken."

Her hand was on his shoulder. So comforting, so soothing. He'd forgotten how much he'd missed the reassurance of another person's caring touch. He trained his gaze on the twinkling sparkles of light, dewy pastures by moonlight, lit like a far-away fairy kingdom, all make-believe.

"Fabiana told me that my father abandoned my mother and me when I was only two years old," he said.

Patience's hands came firmer on his shoulder. "Surely your father wondered what became of you. You should seek him and talk to him."

"He should seek me. I'm his son. He abandoned me."

There it was, the familiar ache and loneliness pushing out Luca's anger. Every time he thought himself rid of the anger, memories haunted him. He was a child with no parents, no one who truly cared. In thirty years, no one had greeted him in the morning with a warm cup of tea when he awoke, or wished him good night when he retired for the evening to his lonely tent.

"The marquess has been an acquaintance for many years," Patience said. "He's one of the few nobles whom I respect."

"He's a good-for-nothing with a cold heart."

Patience's hands glided across Luca's shoulders in the same way she might soothe a caged tiger. "Now that I look at you, your resemblance to your father is astounding. Your height, the angle of your chin, all remarkably the same. Indeed, your skin is darker, but little else. No one will refute your claim as his heir."

Luca jerked away from her hands. "I have no claim. And if

I did, my only claim is that he's a loathsome man and I don't want him as a father. He deserted my mother and me."

"His desertion, for whatever reasons, forced you to become a stronger man."

"If a strong man starves and begs to feed his tribe winter after winter, then I'm very strong indeed."

Patience's huge eyes grew contemplative, the skin beneath smeared with darkened circles. Moonlight came through the window, illuminating the cruel scar on her face, the sprinkle of freckles on her nose and cheeks, making her appear much younger than any image he'd ever harbored of a dowager countess.

"There's much I want to understand about you and your life," she said.

He cupped her face and smoothed the puffiness beneath her eyes. He had no intention of telling her more about himself, because he'd sully her sweetness.

"You should get some sleep," he said.

"Regrettably, I'm more awake now than I was at midnight while I was waiting for you." She cast a sidelong glance at the window. "I can arrange a meeting with your father. To have peace in your life, first you must find it in your heart to forgive."

"How shall I introduce myself at this meeting? We have naught in common. He spends his days practicing his manners, I spend my days practicing survival. Shall I limp into his drawing room as a cripple, dependent on a walking stick?"

"Introduce yourself as the man you are. Valiant, decisive, and daring. You're a leader of a tribe. You're a legend in your own right."

Luca smiled. "People believe I have no weaknesses, although I do have one."

Her face showed a front of humor and disbelief. "You, the legend, admit to a weakness?"

He quirked a brow, then gently kissed her. "Only one, and she soothes my spirit like no one else can."

Patience's hands rested on his shoulders. He breathed in her familiar fragrance, fresh and clean, all lavender and sunshine, despite the dreariness of a cold night.

"Someday I'll bring you a frock the color of the sea, strung with shiny blue beads to match your eyes," he said.

She was purity and unaffected elegance, kind-hearted and glorious, and she'd touched his heart each time she smiled, each time she cared for him.

The low-burning candles on the mantel cast a warm glow on her stunning face. Without warning, she shivered, her eyes tormented. Her expression clouded.

He glanced at the fire in the fireplace, now little more than ashes, and grabbed her hands. "What troubles you, *kamadiyo?*"

"There are memories in this chamber," she said softly. "Hiding under the eaves, summoning to mind cutting insults." Her complexion turned so pale to be almost ethereal, her forehead so tight as to make her thoughts transparent.

Luca squeezed her hands and stared at her. "I'll destroy the memories by slaying them."

The depths of her eyes shimmered a satiny blue before she dropped her gaze to the floor. "Because of my scar, I'm embarrassed when you look so intently at me."

He pressed a kiss to her cheek, to that very same pale disfigurement. "I like to look at you."

She kept her eyes lowered. "I'm plain."

"You're beautiful." He glanced at her slight, dainty hands, and pulled her hands to his. She was so delicate. Protective-ness for her had taken a firm place in his chest. "Roma aren't ashamed of scars. It's part of you and your life."

A crimson blush tinted her freckled white skin. Life with her took away the pain of seeing his father, of endless brawls with nameless faces over his mixed heritage, of long years of loneliness and seeking.

"You'll never abuse me in any way? Not even if you're terribly angry?" She shook her head. "Both men that I've been with have hurt me—my late husband and my...smooth-talking cousin."

Lightly, Luca touched the scar on her cheek. "Is your cousin the man who caused this scar?"

She nodded. "Aye."

He swallowed the prickly lump that had taken up residence in his throat. and guided her to a side chair. "*Kamadiyo,* I'll never hurt you." Retrieving some silk pillows at the foot of the bed, he buoyed the pillows behind her and sat on the floor at her feet.

"'Tis almost dawn," he said. "Try to sleep for a while."

The hours before daybreak went on in a blend of dozing and wakefulness. Lost in thought, he watched her as she slept. She was *wuzho.* Pure and untainted. And, she was the woman he'd been seeking all his life.

CHAPTER TWENTY-EIGHT

*C*rispin departed two days after the dinner with Luca's father. He'd vowed to return within two months. Luca stayed in Patience's attic, knowing that Pulko had grown into a capable leader and could manage the tribe. Every evening, Luca tried to help Patience figure out how to fight charges if Crispin followed through with his threat.

As Luca did each morning, he strode the large expanse of lawn, keeping himself hidden from the servants. Then he found Amelia and Penham sitting together in the kitchen.

He greeted them as he always did, then asked, "Where is Lady Patience?"

"She's somewhere near the stables," Penham replied.

"I'll find her," Luca said.

"Penham will fetch her!" Despite her outburst, Amelia's face waxed deliberately blank when Luca glanced at her. She darted a nervous look at Penham. Without actually acknowledging each other, the two servants seemed to share a private conversation.

"Is there any trouble I should know about that may have happened last evening?" Luca asked carefully.

"Nay!" Both servants shouted in unison.

The lengthening silence was interrupted only by the clank of a rolling pin and the clip of a knife.

"Perhaps I should bathe while I'm waiting for Patience," Luca said.

Amelia rounded on Penham. "Go to the well to fetch buckets of water. then bring a tub to the attic."

"What a bossy woman." Penham cast his knife to the table and trudged out the door.

Amelia set a plate on the table filled with sticky roasted quail, along with a slab of brown bread and a cup of hot tea. Luca bowed his head for a silent prayer, then ate his fill. When he finished, she poured a bowl of creamy custard before him.

While he enjoyed his custard, Amelia grabbed a stool next to him. She pulled off the linen bandages and cleansed his wound, then carped non-stop about the lack of dependable servants and Penham's inability to complete any chore without her detailed instructions.

"Really?" Luca interjected good-naturedly whenever she paused, although it wasn't a question, just a way to feign interest in the conversation.

"Lady Blakwell confided several matters to me last night." The stark change from Amelia's light-hearted chattering to one of quiet gravity was as startling as her normally abrupt change of topics.

"Go on." He tried to respond nonchalantly.

"My lady told me that the Marquess of Wottingham is your father and she wants you and him to meet and resolve your differences."

"He's held no position of value in my life, nor any position at all," Luca pushed back his stool. He forestalled any additional confidences by putting up his hand and striding out the kitchen doorway. He slipped into the kitchen garden, rubbed Oliver's ears, and passed Penham heaving a bucket of water.

"I'll carry it," Luca volunteered to the elderly servant. With a sidewise smile for Amelia and a lengthy, labored breath at the persistent throbbing in his leg, he hoisted the bucket, added a shard of bar soap and several linen cloths, and started up the stairs.

Once in the attic, he grinned to see the tub already partially filled with water. Penham was apparently faster than Luca. A warm afternoon sun streamed through the window. After a trip to the bedchamber below to attend to his needs, he climbed the stairs back to the attic, stripped off his clothes and settled into the bath. He bent his legs to accommodate his long form, washed himself, and scrubbed his hair. When the bath was ended, he dried with a linen towel and pulled clean clothes from his pouch.

As he finished dressing, Patience rushed into the attic and latched the door behind her. She presented a lovely vision. Her color was high, her loose, deep-red hair flying from her shoulders, her luminous blue eyes shining with elation.

He held out his arms and she hurried into them.

Later, he'd remember thinking that her hips seemed ever more rounded then he'd noticed before.

She flung her arms around his shoulders and buried her face in his chest. "You're my Gypsy knight. My perfect dream. Truly, you are a gift from God."

The scent of her satiny, lavender-smelling skin made his blood gallop. Each bend of her delicate limbs, each tender murmur of delight in his ear, was a sound reminder of why he'd returned. He tipped her face and tiny droplets of water remaining on his hands from the bath wet her cheeks.

"How fares your leg today?" she asked.

"Much, much better every day." He was such a cool liar, but he wanted to protect her from worrying about him.

She massaged the clean hair of his scalp and finger combed the wet tendrils from his forehead. Her eyes were perceptive and fun-loving. Her lips were full, a lovely shade of pink.

"Amelia bound my wound in the kitchen and prattled endlessly," he said.

Patience's hands stilled, her demeanor sobered. "You spoke with Amelia...endlessly?"

She bent her head and stared at the bar of soap floating in the tub. He sensed, rather than saw, her mercurial changeover. She kept her eyelids lowered, her fringe of ginger lashes sweeping across her cheekbones. "How long did you converse?" she added.

"Both Amelia and Penham greeted me in the kitchen, as they usually do. Then Penham went to the well and Amelia chattered without a breath while I ate."

"What did Amelia chatter about?" Patience asked.

"As is her way, she complained about Penham and the other servants," Luca replied guardedly. "Why?"

"I wondered if she told you anything else in particular." Patience stepped away to stand by the fireplace. She fingered the neck lacings of her crimson frock. Should he go to her, take her in his arms and demand answers, or should he remain where he was, by the dirty, tepid bathwater, and give her the distance she obviously needed?

"Are you not happy I'm here with you?" he ventured.

She turned from him and faced the fireplace. "Of course. Unbearably happy."

But.

She hadn't uttered the word but her anxiety weighted the very air of the room.

Guardedly, he walked to her. He stood close but not touching, within arm's reach. In case she decided to break away, he could grab her quickly.

"Look at me," he ordered.

She turned slowly. If she was so 'unbearably happy,' the excitement and laughter had long disappeared from her face. Her whole demeanor had shifted, becoming apprehensive and serious. Her naturally radiant complexion was drawn and pale, the freckles fairly jumping from her skin.

This close, he had to touch her. He lightly stroked his knuckles across her smooth cheeks. She froze and briefly closed her eyes.

"I cannot fix what I don't understand." He caught her shoulders, pressed his lips against her hair. "No problem is too great that we can't find a solution together. You know that I'll not allow Crispin to take you to London."

"This isn't about Crispin." She shifted in his arms. "And I fear you'll never accept this one."

He massaged her shoulders, his thumbs kneaded the tight muscles in her back. He took some satisfaction from the fact that she let him hold her.

"Several months ago," he began, "when I was helpless, I promised I'd protect you because I was indebted to your kindness, remember? Please tell me what's wrong." His hands grazed her sleeves, leaving imprints of his damp fingertips along her shoulders.

She winced and shrank back.

He lifted his hands. "When have you ever been repelled by my touch?"

"'Tis not your touch." Inching forever backward, she eyed him cautiously. She reached the wall, which prevented her from retreating. Frowning, she pressed her palms so hard on either side of herself that her knuckles whitened. "'Tis just that my skin has become more and more sensitive and tender."

Sensitive? Tender? Why?

Suspicion and mistrust screamed through him. The peculiar way Amelia and Penham had behaved. Luca scrambled for suitable reasons for their evasive behaviors, suitable rationales.

"I was gone so often..." He shook his head, thoughts colliding, then strode to her and seized her forearms. "Who is he?"

"How dare you accuse me of behaving as if I were one of your Gypsy strumpets."

Luca's mind shouted, refusing to believe she wanted another man, while his heart fractured into tiny pieces. "You don't lie well, despite your Christian ways."

She leaned against the door. "Take your hands off me."

He loosened his grip. He ached to thrust her traitorous, trembling self away from him as much as he ached to hold her close and feel the exquisite beating of her heart.

She forced him to look at her by brushing her fingers along his tight jaw. And in that moment he knew one thing for certain. She hadn't found another man when he'd returned to his tribe. No woman, however blameworthy, could weave such an expression of indignant fury and confusion, then be so devoted to him since his return.

He slowed his breathing until a breadth of calmness returned and he could see another color besides blood-red anger.

"I'm simply possessive of the woman who has taken away my heart," he admitted.

Her delicate eyebrows snapped together. "Don't blame your outrageous temper on me." She marched to the paned window.

He scraped his hands over his face and blew through his fingers. "I can blame my temper on the fact that I'm a Rom, but in truthfulness, 'tis because I'm hopelessly in love with you."

He didn't know what he'd expected from his admittance

because he'd surprised himself for declaring his thoughts aloud.

She swiveled. "And I love you, my Richard the Lionheart."

"Then what's wrong? Everyone seems to know except me."

She stared at the toes of her flat shoes, decorated with a delicate purple bow. "I planned to explain everything later this evening, after I'd finally admitted the truth to myself." She sighed heavily. "Since we first met, you've been concerned that you'd become a cripple, but you should be more concerned about your eyesight, because you're most certainly blind."

She kept her gaze out the paned glass window. Then she splayed her hands protectively over her stomach and gazed out into the deepening dusk.

Luca stood where he was and waited for her to speak.

"Do you know the color of my eyes?" Her voice was low, a rustling whisper with a suspiciously sharp edge.

"Your eyes are blue. As blue as the salty blue sea."

"When you look at me, who do you see?"

"The woman of my dreams," he answered immediately. "The woman I want as my wife."

There was a sharp intake of her breath, followed by a mountain of quiet. Although her back was to him, he knew she'd heard his proposal of marriage. Yet when she turned, her expression was unreadable.

"Do you like children?" she asked.

This was definitely the day for the most unusual questions.

"Aye. The Rom adore children." Luca reached her in three panther-like strides. He cupped his hands around her shoulders. "Why? *Why?*"

She swallowed, seeming to push back tears. After several efforts to speak, she choked, "I'm reassured to hear this."

The scent of sun-dried grass wafted through the window. Tawny pinks and pale orange from the day's end sun filtered through the window and illuminated her fair skin. This near, he admired the sapphire flecks in her eyes despite the clash of emotions they conveyed.

He fumbled for answers. "Is there a child in the village who's ill? Are you ill?"

She gave him a quiet smile. "I didn't mean to worry you."

"Shall I summon Amelia?" he asked.

"Many lady's maids would need to be summoned throughout England for many English ladies because my illness is quite ordinary." She shook her head and sighed. "For some time, I've missed my monthly flux."

"Monthly—"

"I am with child."

Instantly, one question came to mind. How, because the child couldn't be his?

All the air flew from his body. He tried to draw a clear, full breath, but his lungs wouldn't cooperate. Somewhere from his lost youth, an image came to mind of the child he'd imagined he might be blessed with. He gazed at Patience, visualizing that precious child they'd one day have together—with dark freckled skin, black unruly hair, and eyes the color of sapphires.

"I suspected a while ago, but I waited. When I missed my fourth month, my suspicions were confirmed."

He heard her words, said so softly that they didn't enter the reasoning portion of his brain.

Luca gazed at her, at her body.

Dreadfully calm, he waited. But somewhere in his heart he already knew. God help him, he already knew.

"I've suspected for a while now." She turned. She had the agitated stiffness of a woman conflicted by both joy and sorrow. "I carry my late husband's child."

CHAPTER TWENTY-NINE

*I*t was if she'd struck her fist into his stomach, for the physical suffering was as great as the anguish in his mind. He was breaking into small pieces. Pieces that tore through his insides, accelerating to a tempo and intensity that cut off all rational breath.

He should speak. He didn't react quickly enough. Her words hummed in his brain, her mouth worked in slow motion.

Luca dragged air into his chest and swallowed a deluge of disbelief and lost dreams.

"Your late husband's child. I planned to marry you and all the while you carried your late husband's child. An English child." He shambled to a nearby wooden chair, gripping the wood until his hands were bloodless.

"I feared this might be your reaction," she said. "Knowing the type of man you are—so proud of your customs and loyal to your Gypsy heritage, harboring such ill will toward the English. But I'd hoped you might be happy, at least for me."

He closed his eyes. Frustration and regret didn't allow him to speak.

A better man might've assured her that, indeed, he was quite happy for her. Delighted, in fact. So delighted that he still planned to wed her. So delighted that he'd raise her child as his own, this full-blooded English child who wasn't his.

But he wasn't a better man. He was a half-blood, a destitute man. A man who stole as a way of life, who fought in the dirt with his fists, not atop a prancing black horse. He was a man who'd fibbed and falsified all sorts of tales to the *gadje*, and, aye, laughed at them afterward for their stupidity. But in reality, he'd played a serious game he needed to win every time to survive.

He blew a deep audible breath and opened his eyes. "I'm not an English gentleman, forever polite and chivalrous."

"I know who you are."

"Do you?" He refused to meet her gaze. "Then you know me better than I know myself."

She went to him and touched his chin, forcing him to look at her. "You're kind and tender."

Misery and fury clustered around him like flies and he swatted at the empty air. "Did you expect a more joyous response to your happy news?"

"Congratulations are in order."

"Congratulations, Lady Blakwell."

"Thank you, Monsieur Boldor." She seemed to chuckle at the ridiculous formality. "Or Monsieur Wottingham?"

"Boldor. I take my mother's surname."

Patience drew a long sigh. "For years, I'd prayed for a child to love, to give me hope when I was alone and afraid, living on this wretched estate."

"The birth of a child is always a reason for celebration," Luca said coolly, carefully. He reached for his boots and cloak, cinched the green sash about his waist.

"Will you not stay—at least until the morrow?" He sensed she wouldn't allow him to leave until he answered, for he recognized the real meaning of her question. All he had to do was change the words.

Will you not stay—permanently, as you promised?

He shrugged into his cloak. "I need time alone."

Her face was as pale as frosted marble, her eyes beseeching. A fortnight ago, a sennight ago, indeed, this very day, she'd called him her perfect dream. Her Gypsy knight. Her gift from God.

But he was a far cry from her dreams, and she could never comprehend his reality.

His Romany life spanned thirty years. His new English experiences, this new English love, this utterly English child, all were a mere speck in the scope of his lifetime.

"Where's the man who wanted to marry me?" she asked quietly. "The Gypsy who vowed to protect me from my unspeakable burdens?"

"He refuses to fight a battle he cannot win."

"Then he's not a true champion if he expects an easy victory. The man I know welcomes a challenge. He's a legend."

Luca wasn't feeling particularly like a legend. He felt numb and tired. He flexed the cramp in his leg and wondered if it was conceivable to feel anything other than pain ever again. Under impossible choices, he was fast becoming a man he neither understood nor respected. He was fast becoming a man like his father, who refused to accept the responsibility of a child.

"I've fought many battles, Lady Blakwell," he said. "A true victor knows his opponent, even when he's outnumbered. But I'm defenseless against a man under a gravestone."

"The man I love is no coward."

"Each time I see the child's English face I'll be reminded of my utter loathing of the English. If the child was between me and you, that would've been wonderful. You're the rare, good English person. But knowing this child is the progeny of a typically cruel one..."

"The child of whom you speak is *my* child, too."

Luca threw his pouch over his shoulder, chancing a glimpse at her as he strode to the door. He knew she'd honed the art of keeping her features unruffled despite her ordeals, except now her face was devoid of any emotion except exposed, raw pain.

~

*A*fter all the servants had retired for the evening. Patience found Luca later that night in the drawing room. He stood by a low burning fire in the fireplace, staring into the bluish flames. Only one beeswax candle was lit along the sideboard, offset by the glow thrown by the smoky oil lamps near the entry. Absorbed by the fire, he didn't seem aware that she'd entered.

She sucked in a breath, along with her pride, and went to him.

Lightly, she touched his shoulders. "I feared you'd left without saying goodbye."

He shook her off and raised his hand in a mock salutation. "But here I am, your ever-present servant, owned by you, bound to this dower house. Or rather, owned by the Rom, bound to the tribe." He smiled, seeming to appreciate the irony coloring his words. "I may yet fight so I can find what I've been seeking all my life."

She wanted to rub her fingers along his arm, but something in his eyes filled her with apprehension. She hesitated, then stiffened her spine.

"Seeking what? Seeking whom?" she asked.

Luca glanced toward her and she saw, for a moment, a

hopeful, vulnerable boy in his bloodshot eyes, before life had dealt him inconceivable hardships and poverty.

From behind one of the benches she retrieved a walking stick and held it out to him. "I found this in the attic. Amelia must've made another one for you."

The joke didn't amuse, for his black eyes glittered. "I have no use for it."

She tried again, to initiate a conversation with him, any conversation. "Pulko was here earlier," she began.

"I know. I spoke with him."

She looked down at her hands and swallowed. "I caught him stealing from the pantry. He said your tribe lacked mustard for the cod, and ginger for the port wine he'd swindled from a noble. When I inquired further, he admitted he'd stolen from me for months, and that you knew. I wondered where so much of the food went."

"How did you expect my tribe to eat while I ailed?"

"I didn't mind, but why did you never tell me? If I could, I would've sent more."

His angry silence burned the air in response. She surveyed the bleak, forbidding outline of his profile and her breath trapped in her chest. Moments like these reminded her of how intimidating he and his mysterious life were. She swallowed bravely. "You didn't want to tell me because of your insufferable pride. You didn't want to admit you needed to depend on someone other than yourself."

"I'll repay any stolen food. I'm not a criminal."

She set the walking stick by the fireplace. Then she stepped nearer to this unfeeling stranger who looked like Luca, talked like Luca, but surely couldn't be the man she loved. His shiny black hair was disheveled. His linen shirt was untucked, his orange scarf and green sash thrown to the floor.

"I want to speak about my baby. Our baby," she said.

"We have no baby." His forehead furrowed, the thought

seeming to take every ounce of concentration. "You have a baby."

"There's still the matter of Crispin's threats hanging over us, but I want you to be the father of my baby."

"Unfortunately, that title is already bestowed upon your late husband, Lord Bertram Blakwell."

She dragged air into her tight lungs. "I want you as the true father. I want my baby to know you, learn from you, and love you as I do."

He sank his head to his hands. "You don't want me as a father. I'm the spawn of a malicious man."

Her fingers smoothed the bump on his nose. "Your father is agreeable and well-respected. I've known him for years."

Luca tried to stand, wobbled, and dropped back to the settee. "Once, you asked me once how my nose was broken."

She felt as if she were in a dream and didn't know how to answer. "I assumed you were in a brawl."

"A brawl. A simple brawl. How easily I could defend myself against an equal opponent. Sadly, I harbor a child's hazy memory."

She envisioned him, a sturdy toddler covered in mud, showing off skinned knees and scraped elbows to any tribesman who feigned interest. Shoving up his tattered sleeves and challenging any foe with tiny, upraised fists.

"Did you try to fight the biggest bully in the tribe?" she teased.

"I was pushed."

"Were you pushed by Marko?" she asked.

"I was pushed into the dirt by my esteemed father." Luca shook his head, a seemly attempt to clear the film of sadness on his face. "I remember that my mother had quarreled with him."

Patience went still, a chink of steel heavy in her belly.

Very softly, very gently, she said, "Go on."

"My father said he was leaving. I ran after him, called out to him. I grabbed his leg as he walked and he pushed me—pushed me so hard I toppled and broke my nose. I still remember how the blood tasted, like sticky metal on my tongue. I remember Fabiana screaming, my mother crying, a brown bird in a birdcage chirping gaily, oblivious to the cruelty."

Holding back tears, Patience said, "You said the memory was hazy."

Luca shook his head. "My father didn't care about my cries. He walked out of my life, out of my mother's life. Fabiana told me they'd quarreled because he didn't want me. I was so dark, so different from him. How could he be proud of a Romanes son?" Luca raised his shoulders in a gesture of indifference. "It matters naught. I no longer care."

"I think," she said softly, "you care a great deal."

"My father resented my mother and me. We'd trapped him in our world and he missed his comfortable English life. My bitterness toward the English will rail against your English child."

"Never. You're a man of principle. You rely on a childhood memory that may not be true."

"Fabiana wouldn't lie. She took me in and raised me after my mother died."

"Fabiana may be harboring her own hatred against the English for her own reasons."

"I won't pull you nor your child into my Romany world."

Patience lifted her hands to feel his face, his hair. "I want your world. Once we're wed, I want your children."

But he was faster than she, even now his expression clearing. He looked around. "You enjoy your English finery. You refused to live in a Rom tribe. You claim you want my world, although 'tis under your conditions."

"Your opinion of me is low and unwarranted. You know I

can't leave while my despicable stepson holds this murder charge over my head."

Luca stood. "Aye."

"You're leaving?" she asked. "I thought you were going to protect me against Crispin."

Luca rubbed his hands across his face and didn't answer.

She waited a few moments, feeling a slow anger simmering inside her. When Luca didn't respond, she grabbed the walking stick, advanced, and slammed the stick into Luca's stomach. Besides an oomph and particularly strong Romanes words, he hardly moved.

She threw the stick to the floor and charged out of the drawing room. At the doorway, she swerved. "Do what you do best, Mr. Boldor. Dash off as soon as things get too difficult. I'll face this obstacle, as I've face every obstacle in my life, on my own."

A storm brewed in his gaze, flashing across his face like a whirlwind.

"You're a coward who can't be trusted to keep his word," she said. "Wander the whole wretched world like a nomad and take care of your tribe if Pulko needs help, which he doesn't. Just leave me a modest bit of pride and keep away from Ipswich." Her fists tightened. "I had begun to believe that you were a trustworthy man who truly cared, but you're like every other man. I love this baby. I don't need your protection against Crispin nor Marko, nor your meaningless proposals of marriage." Sobs welled and she fought hard to contain them, years and years of sobs, like a torrent with no beginning nor end.

The color leached from Luca's face. His eyes were glazed, a tortured man calling for help, for patience. "*Kamadiyo,* I don't know what to do when a woman cries."

"'Tis easy." She licked at the tears on her upper lip. "Get out!"

"Marko's on his way toward the sea and may be heading toward my tribe. When Pulko came earlier, he said there may be bloodshed. He can't fight Marko's tribe alone."

"Then you must hurry to depart." She swiped at her face, could hardly breathe. "Be sure to take all of your belongings—your clothes, your scarf, your cloak." She felt sick, her fingers tingled with cold. She tried to keep her shoulders straight, her manner dignified.

It would be the last time he saw her, and she didn't want to be remembered as a sniveling, woebegone fool. Furiously, she sniffed and brushed a final tear from her cheeks. Her hands were shaking terribly.

He reached for her. For a wild moment she thought of grabbing his fingers, begging him to stay.

"I'll leave at first light," he said. "I'll come back after—"

She thrust his hands away. Iron replaced her bent spine. "Go back to the Rom. 'Tis where you belong."

CHAPTER THIRTY

*P*atience stood by her bedchamber window while her dog slept by the hooded fireplace. Now and then the dog stretched, yawned, and regarded her with a curious stare.

As she did most days, she stared out the window at the vast, open fields to await the dawn. But this dawn was different. The man she loved was walking out of her life for good.

She shivered, knowing the heat from the fire wouldn't warm her.

She attempted to wrench Luca from her heart, from her mind, by doing what she always did. She swallowed her feelings by burying them at the bottom of her heart where nothing could hurt her. But her stubborn mind insisted on torturing, dredging up his hurtful words.

'Did you expect a more joyous response to your happy news?'

She squeezed her eyes shut to stop the flood of desolation. Self-righteous anger, like a defensive dam, barred her from drowning in self-pity.

Luca. Her trustworthy protector. Her beloved. Just the

thought made her broken heart laugh. Her cynical, shattered, broken heart.

She swabbed her eyes with the back of her hand. She had to forget him. With the grace of God, she had to look forward and find a way to defend herself against Crispin's coercion.

But Luca's tenderness flooded her with memories.

'Kamadiyo, you're beautiful.'

She held these memories close, for they calmed the empty place in her heart. Once, he'd been taken with her. She remembered his warm scent of buckskin and exotic spices whenever he stood near.

Her. Skinny, plain, as ordinary as a gray church mouse. They could never be together as Luca and Patience because there was no Patience. That young girl with wide-eyed dreams had become lost a long time ago. For a while with him, she thought she was truly alive, that she'd enjoy a wondrous life, filled with his love.

Luca was a proud, Gypsy man. His Romany beliefs were firmly imbedded in his nature.

She continued to gaze out the window and her heart did a flip when Luca came into the field, staying low and out of sight. His steps were slow and uneven. A chilly spring wind sent a thin mist of rain through the branches and the trees bent. He glanced at her window and for a moment she thought he'd call out. She stepped away so he wouldn't see her.

She thought to walk downstairs, or take up her sewing. She stayed still, ever patient, her hands on her round stomach, sneaking glances at him through the curtains.

She rendered him free to return to his Gypsy life. No regrets. No trust. No protection. Resentfulness burned, filling Patience's veins with unwanted animosity. She pressed her eyes with her forefingers, refusing to weep. Then she stepped to her wingback chair by the fireplace and sat alone, the land-scape of her life.

She dozed. An hour later, she glanced at the window. An unusual flickering of torches on the main road leading to the dower house made her pause. It was too early for the maid-of-all-work to awaken as it was not yet half past five o'clock in the morning. The sound of carriage wheels crunched on the ground.

Patience moved to the window and pressed her face to the glass. Two horses blasting great puffs of steam through their nostrils stopped at the front of the house.

A few moments passed, and the beginning measures of a Haydn Sonatina tinkled on the keys of the pianoforte. More moments, then Crispin's shrill voice sounded from the hall.

Oliver scampered to her bedchamber door and growled. Patience dressed in her morning frock and tied a warm shawl around her shoulders. As soon as she opened the bedchamber door, the dog raced through the hallway and down the stair-well. She rushed after him in time to see Oliver scrabble into the kitchen.

Her stepson, Digby, and Marko stood together in the hall-way. She couldn't breathe. She glanced at the stairwell, wondering if she'd make it up the stairs in time to get away from them.

"How lovely you look." Crispin spoke first. "No introduc-tions are in order, as you already have met Marko. He and I came across each other in London."

She looked anything but lovely after a night of weeping. She caught a glimpse of herself in the window's reflection. Her nose was red, her face pale as death, the lines of sadness etched below her mouth.

So this was how it must be. Men who were once strangers, banding together against her. If she had any doubt they were up to evil, all she need do was gaze at their grim faces and the hard glint in their stares.

Crispin removed his top hat and tucked it under his arm. "'Tis rumored you consorted again with a Gypsy man." He waved an accusing finger. "Scandal will never do if you expect to win your case against me in court."

Marko mopped his sweaty face with a dirty handkerchief. His thick fingers were scarred, the tiny yellow flares from his eyes ferocious. "Luca will come with me."

"He's not here," she said.

Marko stepped closer. The memory of his cruelty immobilized her.

"He was here," she clarified, "but he left."

Foolishly, she threw a fleeting glimpse toward the door and Marko's suspicious scowl followed her. She averted her gaze to the kitchen and saw movement. Most likely Oliver cowered behind the cupboards with the maid-of-all-work.

"Where are my other servants?" she demanded of Crispin, to keep the men talking and occupied until she thought of a way to escape.

"I sent Penham and Amelia on a fool's errand to the village for supplies," Crispin said.

"Why do you want to hurt me with these false murder accusations?" she asked.

Crispin pushed back his shoulders, looking the foolish fop from his gold-buckled shoes to his yellow satin cravat. "I want to protect my inheritance. I plotted my father's killing and paid Italian bandits a handsome sum to do the deed. My father hoarded his riches. Old men like him live forever."

"Why did you blame me for his death?"

"You were a convenient suspect. When I was in London, I often played the pianoforte and thought of my father constantly ridiculing me. He said men didn't play the pianoforte, only women. Nonetheless, I was the real man in the end because I had the last say."

"Your father ridiculed everyone," she said.

Crispin smiled. "Then I heard from a former scullery maid several months ago, that the servants suspected you might be pregnant because you'd complained about feeling nauseated. I knew the child was my late father's. I've waited a long time for my inheritance and no stepbrother or sister will jeopardize it. I know what your father had written in the marriage contract and that a certain amount of money would be set aside for any children. This, I assure you, won't happen. You'll travel to London with me when Marko is finished with you."

"Try it." Luca stood in the kitchen doorway, looking like fury himself. "Any of you."

Patience whirled as Digby lunged for her. She dodged him, lost her footing, and collided with the balustrade near the stairwell. Digby clamped his hands around her shoulders and her muscles shook with the effort of trying to hold still. If he jerked her forward, she'd fall face-first to the floor and she might lose her baby if she was injured.

Two pulses of aggression and violence, Marko and Crispin, intercepted Luca midway in his flight to reach her. Marko caught Luca's ankles.

Luca reeled. Crispin kicked him to the floor, leaned over Luca, and held down his arms.

Marko seized the walking stick by the fireplace. He took aim and swung at Luca's kneecap. The hall exploded with the sickening snap of solid wood smashing into bone and muscle.

"Needing this to walk, aye? Becoming a simpering cripple, like a *gadje*?" Marko shouted, punching again and again at Luca's leg.

Patience's heartbeat maddened, her limbs trembling uncontrollably in Digby's grip. She heard herself screaming

Luca's name, tracking the horrible scene as if it were performed in slow motion.

Luca moaned, his body jerked. The dagger fell from his hand and skidded across the floor. His left leg twisted helplessly. His buckskin breeches grew red, then black with blood.

Oliver charged into the hall. Crispin's grip loosened on her as he tripped over the dog. With a heroic leap and a bar of pointed canine teeth, the dog bit into Marko's swinging arm. Oliver held his bite, tiny in contrast, attached to the mammoth Gypsy.

For a stunned second, Marko cursed savagely. He dropped the walking stick and wrenched the offending dog from his arm. "What vile, evil spirit is this?" He flung the dog to the floor. Whimpering, Oliver's tiny pink tongue protruded from his mouth and his eyes lost their sheen. Blood coursed from the side of his small, shaggy body.

Patience lurched free from Digby. She tore across the hallway to her dog and took Oliver in her arms.

Luca rolled, then drove his fists into Marko's husky chest. Marko's legs buckled. A table crashed and shattered while splinters flew through the air. A vicious strike from Crispin sent Luca sprawling.

Patience's high-pitched cries stuck in her throat. She made a move to stand and met Digby's enraged eyes and unforgiving grip. "You're becoming more and more of an inconvenience, Lady Blakwell."

"As are you." Brandishing a gun, Pulko strode into the room and pointed it at Digby.

The muscles in Digby's veiny neck stood out and his jaw slackened. He vanished into the shadows of the hallway.

Patience huddled her dog to her chest. "Pulko, thank God —." She wanted to say more, but dizziness spun around her.

The constable of a neighboring town, short and thin with

a ripple of blonde whiskers, trotted into the room behind Luca's father.

"Put that gun down, you filthy troublemaker!" the constable shouted at Pulko.

With noticeable reluctance, Pulko lowered the gun.

Luca's father assisted Patience to a side chair in the dining room. Then he turned to Luca, then Marko, then Pulko. "Who are all these troublemaker Gypsies? Constable, arrest them all."

Luca winced, his right eye bloody and closed. He drew a long-suffering breath. "Father."

CHAPTER THIRTY-ONE

*L*uca's father had been overcome at Luca's address. He'd promptly sent the constable away and admonished Crispin and Digby when the facts emerged. Pulko had returned to Colchester and his tribe by the sea.

A sennight later, Patience perched on a settee in the drawing room with Oliver snuggled in the crook of her arm. A low fire kindled in the grate, enough to take the chilliness out of the air. Bowls of strawberries and clotted cream were set on the dining room table.

Luca occupied the wingback chair near the fireplace. As always, his clothes were a cacophony of colors and styles. She'd mended his linen shirt. His buckskin breeches, slit to the knees, had been laundered several times, the bloodstains a somber reminder of the brutal struggle that had occurred. He'd tied the orange scarf around his throat instead of his hair, giving him a dashing, debonair appearance.

He tendered her with a bemused look. "Sometimes I think you give your dog more notice than me."

"Oliver was injured only a few short days ago."

"As was I," Luca reminded.

"Amelia fretted over your wounds and reapplied her liniment every day."

These were as good excuses as any, because she couldn't bring herself to be too near him. Her emotions were precariously close to the surface.

"My leg healed nicely. 'Twould have been more to my liking, though, if Amelia had tended to Oliver and you had tended to me."

Patience scraped her chair farther from him. "Oliver is my devoted companion and fought off Marko. Oliver is a hero."

Luca raised dark eyebrows. "You can sit nearer, my lady. Unlike your dog, I don't bite."

"Amelia said you requested a roasted hedgehog for dinner, but she decided on roasted pheasant, instead." Inwardly, Patience congratulated herself on changing the direction of the conversation so smoothly.

"We can enjoy roasted hedgehog together next time."

Next time? Surely he jested. There'd be no next time.

He'd told her that he was leaving at first light. Pulko had sent word that Nanosh had visited their tribe. There'd been no fighting, no bloodshed, no attacks. Perhaps peace was met with peace, as God intended.

Luca hadn't explained where he was going, but she assumed he planned to return to his tribe, although Pulko was clearly now the leader.

Luca hadn't mentioned Patience's unborn child. He hadn't mentioned his marriage proposal, although he'd cried off that a sennight ago. Nothing had changed, although she kept her reflections to herself.

She glanced out the window. The afternoon shadows lengthened and the stone arches of the field walls were spangled in streaks of firelight. A groundskeeper was lighting the evening torches earlier than usual in anticipation of their honored guest.

"Are you certain you're ready for your father to dine with us?" she asked.

"I've been ready since I was a babe."

"Good, because he's arrived and we should greet him at the portico." She stood, kissed Oliver's moist black nose, and bundled the dog on a quilt by the fire. To her surprise, the dog shook off the quilt and trotted to the kitchen.

As Patience walked past Luca, he caught her hand. "If my father wants to speak to me, he knows where I am."

At his touch, an uninvited quiver heated her body. She tossed her long ringlets over her shoulder and wrenched her hand free. "Your father helped Pulko find the constable and saved us all," she reminded.

"Soon, I'll need a tally sheet to keep track of all the heroes."

"Because of your father and Pulko, Crispin and Marko will remain in prison a long time. Surely he's worth the effort of a welcome as a sign of respect."

"Perhaps if I could walk on two strong legs, I might reconsider, but I'd be forced to limp in order to greet him properly."

"So limp. It makes no difference."

He met her gaze. "My entire life I resented him, although part of me wanted to prove I'd grown into a man he was proud to call his own."

"And you have."

Luca shook his head. "I'm a cripple forced to take shelter and aid from a woman."

Before Patience could fire a rejoinder, Penham, in his loftiest manner, ushered 'Lord Haringley, Marquess of Wottingham,' into the hallway.

Patience scurried up to greet Luca's father. They reached the drawing room and the marquess removed his top hat and overcoat and handed them to Penham. With noticeable reluctance, Luca grabbed his walking stick and stood.

"Well," Patience said to both men brightly, "I'm certain both father and son wish to speak in private. I'll be outdoors, as my dog is well enough for a walk."

"I like you near me when there are obstacles to confront," Luca murmured.

"You'll need to confront them on your own," she replied.

She walked to the hallway, shrugged on her muslin pelisse, and glanced back. He must've given his features strict orders not to reveal any emotion because his face was bland and she couldn't read his thoughts.

~

*L*uca's gaze settled on the tall, angular man standing across from him. His father wore a squared off blue waistcoat trimmed in sable fur, a silky white cravat around his neck, and sable breeches tucked into black leather boots with tassels. His brown eyes lit with affection.

As Luca stared, the indigo blue coloring of his father's waistcoat became too vibrant, and the drawing room walls seemed to push forward and block the hasty retreat he'd planned if their conversation grew too uncomfortable.

He scratched the stubble on his chin. This reunion with his father—he should've never allowed Patience to talk him into it. Unenthusiastically, he accepted his father's handshake, noting they were the exact same height.

His father kept hold of Luca's hand. "When I realized 'twas you, so horribly beaten by Marko and Crispin, I could hardly breathe. I lost you once. To lose you again would be too much for an old man to accept."

Luca stiffened in surprise, but allowed his father to maintain his grasp. Before his father had entered the hall, he'd decided to feign an obligatory civility, if for no other reason than to appease Patience. His heart still harbored bitterness for this elderly man to allow any new feelings to get in the way of his old ones.

"When did you ever lose me?" Luca asked.

"Fabiana sent word about a year after your mother's death. She said you'd perished while you wandered through the forest and your body was never found." He opened his mouth, closed it. "I was beside myself with grief. First I lost your mother, then I lost my young son."

Luca dropped his hand and stepped back to study his father. "Why would you believe Fabiana?"

"She was your mother's dearest friend." He retrieved a linen handkerchief from his waistcoat and unabashedly wiped at his eyes. "I've lived so many years without you and—"

Luca permitted his father to guide him to the wingback chair. His father settled opposite. An unobtrusive Penham set two cups of tea beside them and quit the room.

"Why did you leave our tribe?" Luca let his question, the question that plagued his entire life, hang between them.

"Your mother ordered me out of the Gypsy camp. She knew I was torn between my English ways and her Gypsy ones. 'Tis my greatest regret, my fatal flaw as a man, not standing beside the woman I loved. My family didn't accept her but I should've fought harder. They threatened to cut off my inheritance. Fool that I was, I bowed to their prejudices, vowing I'd return to her someday. Sadly, I never had the chance."

Aware his jaw hardened as he grimly cast off his father's excuses, Luca charged, "You didn't have the decency to marry my mother."

"On the contrary. Of course I married her. Fabiana was in attendance."

Luca grabbed and squeezed the handle of the delicate

teacup. He took an acrid sip of bitter black tea and swallowed all the wasted years of his life.

"We had a small Gypsy ceremony and I jumped over a broomstick. A *pliashka*, your mother called it," his father said. "My parents said the ceremony wasn't legal, although it was. Now that I've found you, my son, I want to bestow you with your own estate. My other son, Edmund, is your twin brother. He manages my estate in Wiltshire."

Luca sucked down a mouthful of air, trying to get his thoughts to connect. "Fabiana said my twin brother died at birth." He'd believed Fabiana was a trusted friend. How could she have cheated him out of knowing his father and brother?

"Edmund was frail compared to you," his father said. "After your mother and I quarreled that last time, we agreed we could no longer live together. She allowed me to raise Edmund, and I consented as long as I could still see you. A few months afterward, I was told your mother was dead, and that you'd died shortly afterward. I mourned for a long time." He paused, pulled the handkerchief from his waistcoat. "Forgive me. I weep like a child."

Luca said quietly, "I admire you more for weeping, not less."

His father nodded, slow, thoughtful. "Eventually, I remarried, and the woman is English. We've raised your brother, Edmund, as our English son, as my first-born legitimate heir."

"My twin brother is Lord Edmund Haringley of Wiltshire." Luca sank back into the wingback chair, focused on the fireplace, and ironically shook his head. "If he's missing a pair of black hawking gloves with gold initials, tell him I gave them to a friend who needed them more."

"I pray someday you can meet him," his father said. "I should warn you, though, that your brother is quite a hellion if provoked." He sighed. "And he's been a disappointment as I don't approve of his abrasive behavior nor his habits."

Luca took a tentative breath. He strove to find his expressionless mask to place over his face, but it couldn't be found. All this time, he'd had a father, a brother, and a real home.

He turned to his father and saw the sadness and regret in the specks of familiar amber, so much like his own. He shuddered, feeling his body wanting to bolt, refusing this final confrontation. But he needed to breach his bitter walls, because by denying his English heritage, he'd denied a part of himself and he wanted to bring the ill will toward his father to an end. He needed to swallow his monstrous pride.

"Do you recall the last time you saw me?" Luca asked. "I was a toddler. I ran to you and grabbed your leg. I didn't want to let you go."

"When I was with your mother, living as a Gypsy in the tribe, I existed outside reality. There were neither rules nor requirements beyond the daily chore of living. I liked that."

"But not enough to give up a wealthy English life."

"Not enough." Sorrow tapped the earlier joy from his father's face, leaving him as ashen as Patience's white linen. The weariness of carrying his guilt, a heavy iron chain, seemed tight around his neck.

"This isn't the reply I wanted to hear," Luca said.

"I was hot-tempered in those days, as was your mother. We'd agreed that your twin brother, Edmund, would come with me. That last day, he waited for me in my coach with a servant."

"I fell when you pushed me away," Luca said. "My nose was broken."

His father closed his eyes, as if he'd tried to shut out those final images.

"I never knew you were hurt. The Gypsy elders and Fabiana were shouting, cursing—"

Luca wavered, grabbed for his walking stick. "You left us. You left me lying on the ground." He raised his voice at his father, he heard it, but couldn't stop. In a moment, he'd scream his misery.

He breathed deeply. Nay. A Roma man never screamed.

His father stood and steadied Luca. "Before I came here, I visited your tribe. Fabiana's prejudices against the English are still strong. Fortunately, Pulko seems more open-minded and very mature. In their favor, I believe any strong opinions against the English stem more from their love for you rather than any hatred toward English society."

A nerve pulsated in Luca's temple. Consumed with wrath for Fabiana's deceit, he was hardly aware of his father's next words.

"Luca, will you have patience for an old man, who thought he'd lost his son? I'm seeking your forgiveness for deserting you."

Luca paused to be sure his voice wouldn't break when he spoke. He swallowed. "Aye. And please forgive me for my preconceived opinions without knowing all the facts. My opinions were unfair and biased."

And he'd been wrong in so many ways. He'd been obsessed with confronting his father for his wrongdoings. And he'd found him, neither saint nor monster, simply a man trying to do his best.

～

*H*ours later, Luca and his father had scarcely touched their tea. Judging by the shadows, afternoon was well past. He'd nodded at his father's stories, stories of his life, stories of all that Luca had missed. But in truth, he'd hardly listened.

With the next lull in the conversation, Luca grabbed his walking stick and cloak. He excused himself, assuring his father that he'd return with Patience in time for the evening meal. He went through the entryway, past the road, and into the fields. It was an early spring evening, and a cool breeze nipped the air.

He pulled on his cloak and pushed his pace, his steps as brisk as his limp allowed.

She wasn't in the stables, nor the gardens, nor any of the outlying fields.

"Patience," he called.

Had she worn a cloak? He couldn't remember. Surely she was cold and shivering after staying outdoors the entire afternoon.

He neared the crofter's cottage. "Patience?"

He didn't see her at first. A whipple tree, dark greenish-brown branches twisted in the shape of a cross, had hidden her from view.

She was clad in a blue velvet frock, a paisley shawl wrapped around her shoulders. The heady perfume of fresh dirt and green plants filled the air. A crop of pink wildflowers with dotted yellow centers peeked from the earth.

She knelt beside two stone urns, spade in hand, arranging a row of cream and purple flowers. A watering pot sat beside her. Despite the roundness of her body, she looked so small.

His heart cried out at the sight of her. The gray of early evening painted her profile in a pensive hue.

And she was humming.

Humming, after everything she'd endured. That same sweet cadence that had reached him in his darkest nightmares, singing those same cheerful songs of fair maidens and faraway kingdoms.

She'd stood by him with undying courage and faith, all the while her pregnancy took a toll on her body and explained her fatigue. Not once had he tended to her, nor asked if she'd wanted to rest her feet. Not once had he even so much as pulled up a chair for her.

He limped briskly to her. "You sang those songs to me when I was ill."

She kept digging into the moist, fresh earth, tucking fragile seedlings in straight rows, not turning to acknowledge his presence.

"These violets are beautiful," she said. "The flowers bloom splendidly in the spring."

"The flowers can wait."

She placed the spade on the ground and brushed the dirt from her frock. "Stop that."

"I'm sorry if I sound curt. I'm trying to catch my breath after the long walk. I hurried because I need to speak to you."

She turned. "I feel your eyes on me every time you look at me."

She was right, of course. He couldn't keep his gaze off her.

"How was your visit with your father?" She was tending to the flowers again.

Like a marionette, Luca's feet were tied to an imaginary pole, mere inches from her.

"He's a good man. Finally, I found the answers I've sought all my life." Luca knelt beside her. "I have a twin brother, Edmund. He's been raised as an English gentleman."

"How wonderful that you'll never be alone."

"And my father bestowed me with an estate and wealth beyond my wildest imaginings," Luca said.

Those busy hands, packing the soil around each fragile bud. How much attention did wildflowers need? She watered the soil around the flowers and hesitated, holding the watering pot in the air. "I assume you're leaving for your tribe at dawn."

"Nay."

She pressed her lips together and bent to place another flower in the dirt.

Luca lifted her face and gazed at her. She was crying.

Tears gathered beneath her eyes and streamed down her cheeks, a silent, shuddering river. And she hadn't wanted him to see.

He was the man who'd broken her heart, and she hadn't wanted him to see.

He gathered her to his chest. She didn't struggle. He held her close, trying to take in her sadness. "I came to ask your forgiveness." He threaded his fingers through the ringlets of her gleaming hair. "When you needed me most, I abandoned you. Yet when I needed you, you were always with me. While my hours were darkest I heard your voice and your prayers pulling me back to the surface."

She sniffed and looked away.

"You bore the brunt of my bitterness and prejudices." He tipped her head and brushed the tears from her face. Tenderly, he kissed her. "Don't cry, *kamadiyo*, for I become weak-kneed and defenseless. I love you. I love your child. When a man finds a treasure, he'll not relinquish her for the world. I was wrong. Say you'll marry me."

She hardly moved, although she nodded. He felt her heart pounding against her ribs.

"I love you, too," she whispered.

"We can have a proper English wedding or a Romany wedding, a *pliashka*. Are you willing to jump over a broomstick for me?"

Her lips trembled. "Aye."

"We'll wed by the sea and make our home an English home."

"What about your tribe?"

"They're managing very well under Pulko's capable hands. He's proven that he's a proficient and skilled leader. 'Twas my pride that didn't want to admit the truth earlier.

He and Patience sat together in the darkening countryside. After a long while, Luca stood. "'Tis a long walk back to the house and my sore leg dreads the thought."

Instantly, she surged to her feet. "Are you in pain?"

He looked toward the crofter's cottage. "We can rest there for a while. 'Tis private without a maid pounding on the door or a vigilant, shaggy dog settled as a guardian by the entry. My father might wait awhile in the dining room before taking his meal, but eventually he'll realize we were detained."

❧

*H*ours later, Patience and Luca sat together on a blanket in the crofter's cottage. A tidy fire burned in the grate. A soothing, fine rain drizzled on the windows.

She dozed, cradled in his wool cloak, his cravat as a pillow.

"I love you," he murmured.

She opened her sparkling blue eyes and stared up at him. "Are you never tired?"

He laughed. "When do you wish to marry, *kamadiyo*?"

"Perhaps in a few months."

"Next week," Luca said decisively. "We can settle here in Ipswich."

"This dower house holds too many bad memories. We can move to Whitehaven, where my cousin, Faith, and her sister and brother live."

"Or, we can move out of England altogether and settle in Wales," Luca said. "My good friend, Valentina, lives there with her husband."

"When will you see your tribe if we move that far away?"

"The Romany can live anywhere. When you marry a former Roma lord, you also inherit the entire tribe. Be assured Pulko will guide the tribe to Wales so that they can camp near us on occasion."

Patience's eyes clouded. "You truly don't mind relinquishing your leadership? You're a legend."

"A legend is a fable based on a tidbit of fact, *kamadiyo*."

"Now that you mention it, you never told me the meaning of the word."

He chuckled and placed a kiss on each of her cheeks. "Someday, I will tell you, sweetheart."

 he End

A NOTE FROM JOSIE

Dear Friend,

Thank you for reading *Seeking Patience*. I hope you enjoyed it. *Seeking Patience* is the third book in my Inspirational Regency romance "Seeking" series.

The Romany Gypsy culture is complex and fascinating. After researching their traditions and beliefs, I wanted to write stories focusing on bigotry during the Regency era.

My hope is that this story will make you believe in unselfish love and God's grace.

The Romany Inspirational romances begins with Valentina and James in *Seeking Fortune*, and continues with Charity and Daniel in Seeking Charity.

Seeking Rachel, the fourth book in the series, is also available.

Although not part of the Regency Inspirational series, my Tudor short story, *Seeking Catherine*, featuring a Romany Gypsy hero, is always free.

If you loved Seeking Patience as much as I loved writing it, please help other people find *Seeking Patience* by posting your review here, as well as for the 3-book bundle: The Seeking Series

Seeking Patience is available in ebook, paperback, Large Print paperback, and audiobook.

I'd love to meet you in person someday, but in the meantime, all I can offer is a sincere and grateful thank you. Without your support, my books would not be possible.

As I write my next sweet or inspirational romance, remember this: Have you ever tried something you were afraid to try because it mattered so much to you? I did, when I started writing. Take the chance, and just do something you love.

With sincere appreciation,

Josie Riviera

My Spotify Play List for Seeking Patience is here.

Want more Inspirational romances?

Regency:

Seeking Fortune

Seeking Charity

The Seeking Series

Contemporary:

A Love Song To Cherish

A Christmas To Cherish

A Valentine To Cherish

Romance Stories To Cherish bundle

Holly's Gift

HONEY CAKE RECIPE

Easy and delicious, with ingredients you may have on hand:

Ingredients:

- 1 cup white sugar
- 1 cup honey

- 1/2 cup vegetable oil
- 4 eggs
- 2 teaspoons orange zest
- 1 cup orange juice
- 2 1/2 cups all-purpose flour
- 3 teaspoons baking powder
- 1/2 teaspoon baking soda
- pinch of salt
- 1 teaspoon ground cinnamon

Directions:

1. Preheat oven to 350. Grease and flour a 9x13 inch pan.

2. Sift together flour, baking powder, baking soda, salt and cinnamon.

3. In large bowl, combine sugar, honey, oil, eggs and orange zest. Beat in the flour mixture alternately with the orange juice, mixing just until incorporated. Pour batter into prepared pan.

4. Bake in preheated oven for 50 minutes, then cool and enjoy!

ACKNOWLEDGMENTS

An appreciative thank you to my patient husband, Dave, and our three wonderful children.

ABOUT THE AUTHOR

USA TODAY bestselling author, Josie Riviera, writes Historical, Inspirational, and Sweet Romances. She lives in the Charlotte, NC, area with her wonderfully supportive husband. They share their home with an adorable shih tzu, who constantly needs grooming, and live in an old house forever needing renovations.

To receive my Newsletter and your free sweet romance novella ebook as a thank you gift, sign up HERE.

Join my Read and Review VIP Facebook group for exclusive giveaways and ARCs.

To connect with Josie, visit her website and sign up for her newsletter. As a thank-you, she'll send you a free sweet romance novella.
josieriviera.com/

josieriviera@aol.com

ALSO BY JOSIE RIVIERA

Seeking Patience

Seeking Catherine (always Free!)

Seeking Fortune

Seeking Charity

Seeking Rachel

The Seeking Series

Oh Danny Boy

I Love You More

A Snowy White Christmas

A Portuguese Christmas

Holiday Hearts Book Bundle Volume One

Holiday Hearts Book Bundle Volume Two

Holiday Hearts Book Bundle Volume Three

Holiday Hearts Volume Four

Candleglow and Mistletoe

Maeve (Perfect Match)

A Christmas To Cherish

A Love Song To Cherish

A Valentine To Cherish

A Christmas Puppy To Cherish

A Homecoming To Cherish

Romance Stories To Cherish

Aloha to Love

Sweet Peppermint Kisses

Valentine Hearts Boxed Set

1-800-CUPID

1-800-CHRISTMAS

1-800-IRELAND

1-800-SUMMER

The 1-800-Series Sweet Contemporary Romance Bundle

Irish Hearts Sweet Romance Bundle

Holly's Gift

A Chocolate-Box Valentine

A Chocolate-Box Christmas

A Chocolate-Box New Years

A Chocolate-Box Summer Breeze

A Chocolate-Box Christmas Wish

A Chocolate-Box Irish Wedding

Chocolate-Box Hearts

Chocolate-Box Hearts Volume Two

Recipes from the Heart

Leading Hearts

Si khohaimo may patshivalo sar o tshatshim.
There are lies more believable than the truth.
Old Romany saying

ngland 1811

"*B*ury me standing, for I have been on my knees all my life."

Valentina Rupa bowed her head to hear her beloved mother's last words, to see the twitch of her eyes beneath her eyelids, the rise and fall of her chest beneath the thin blankets.

Her mother's breath faded, already settling into the bleak night, already gone.

Unearthly quiet filled their makeshift canopy. The dwindling light from the nearby campfires of their Romany tribe seeped through the canvas.

"*Daj.* Mother ... don't stop speaking." Tears blinded Valentina's eyes, defeated her voice. She focused on her mother's lips, willing her to speak once more. What good did it do to be a *drabardi*, a powerful fortune-teller and healer if she couldn't save her own mother?

Valentina's younger sister, Yolanda, stood beside her. Yolanda coughed violently, then wheezed.

"Please, Daj, it's not your time." Yolanda's hoarse voice faded to a whisper. "Her lips, she's breathing ..."

"Nay, it's the north wind." Valentina peered at the oak tree branches bending against a biting gust, threatening to collapse their crude canopy. Wagon wheels creaked, groaning into the dirt, familiar sounds, yet so distant. Their mother had lived her entire life in the caravan, traveling from village to village. There was no other way for her. Only the way of the Romany.

The air hung thick and heavy, warning of a hailstorm,

stinging Valentina's damp cheeks. She didn't care, didn't bother to wipe them. She hated the weakness of crying. Crying meant loss and loneliness and defeat.

She glanced at Yolanda, noting her ashen face, the stoop of her slight shoulders. "Try to rest for a while."

"I'm not tired." Yolanda rubbed her temples. "Now that both Mother and Father are dead, we're orphans."

"I'll not abandon you." Valentina choked back her fears and crushing uncertainties. She was the older sister. She always took care of Yolanda.

With shaking fingers, she tucked the threadbare blankets around their mother's feeble body, smoothed the wrinkled fabric, and folded the ends back. Neatly, the way her mother liked it done. Tucked, smoothed, folded. Tucked, smoothed, folded.

"Daj, you starved yourself so we could eat. We'd have found the food we needed somehow." Her hands glided purposefully. "Why do the English treat the Rom as if we're animals?"

"Because this is the land of the English," Yolanda said. "They make their own rules."

Long shivers rippled through Valentina's body, a cadence of trepidation and doubt. In a single, deliberate breath, she blew them out.

The friends who'd discreetly stayed out of the way melted in now, coming from their wagons to gather around the deathbed. The sad cries of the caravan penetrated the dusk. Purple-lipped, the elderly, ragged men and women huddled together, stamping their feet to keep away the chill.

With the sleeve of her frayed cotton gown, Valentina wiped her eyes. Her hands were still wet from retrieving water from the river. She'd used the water to bathe her mother, an ironic Romany custom relying on her mother's willingness to go to her death.

Yolanda helped Valentina gather their mother's personal belongings and carried them to the campfire. The flames rose against the night sky and consumed the remnants of their mother's life—a well-worn apron, a silky fringed sash. Their people burned most possessions of the dead, believing the possessions were unclean and defiled the living.

Valentina skimmed her index finger across her mother's double-edged dagger and accidentally drew blood. Grimacing, she licked her finger. She didn't have the heart to destroy the weapon, so she thrust the dagger into its sheath and tied it on a cord along her gown's seam.

Then she slid her palm across the last treasure, her mother's yellow scarf, her *diklo*. Bringing it to her face, Valentina closed her eyes and inhaled. The scent of oak and jasmine, exotic and mysterious, flooded through her. She remembered her mother jauntily tying the diklo around her greying hair each morning.

Valentina knew she was supposed to take one small token before burial, although she took two. She'd never been one to obey rules. She folded the yellow scarf into a perfect triangle and tied it loosely around her throat. It didn't match her faded scarlet gown, and that didn't matter.

Nothing mattered now except her sister.

Yolanda's pretty, round face contorted in grief as she placed small multicolored stones around their mother's body. Valentina inserted pearls in her mother's nose to keep out all wickedness. Her hands wavered, and she avoided touching the body for fear of contamination.

Inhaling the fragrance of a drop of frankincense, she smoothed the spicy golden oil along her arms to protect herself against evil spirits. A shadow of skepticism crossed her soul, and her hands stopped. Maybe spirits didn't exist at all. They certainly demanded endless rituals, and in return granted ... nothing. Glancing around at the eerie silhouettes dancing in the firelight, she dabbed a few more drops of oil on her wrists, just in case.

The men of their tribe had moved to sit in the grassy clearing on the forest's edge, the scent of sweet blackberry brandy filling the brisk October air. They'd stolen it from an unsuspecting Englishman in town. Several grizzled dogs lay listless at their feet.

Luca, the caravan's young leader, was the only man who stood. His baggy green pants were fitted at the ankle and billowed in the wind. He mourned Valentina and Yolanda's mother in a plaintive cadence and guided the elders in solemn chants. Although all the other young men had gone off in search of food and never returned, Luca hadn't deserted the tribe.

"I'll get more hot water, Yolanda, before we prepare for Daj's burial." Valentina retrieved her wool cloak and then hoisted a pot of water off of a smoky campfire. With her free hand, she brushed a strand of hair behind her ear, longing for a warm bath. However, custom prevented her from washing until after her mother's burial.

She made her way past the lamenters to the small tent the women shared. An afternoon rain had washed soggy leaves over the ground. One of the dogs lifted its head and sniffed, the thick fur around its neck bristling. A sudden crackle—somewhere a tree branch snapped.

Her senses sharpened. The last few nights she'd dozed while nursing her mother and had dreamed about a man. A rich man. A powerful man.

Scanning the dense woods, she sensed someone was watching. She had the gift of second sight, her mother had said, but Valentina shook the thought away. Besides, her tribe was far too secluded to be found.

*** End of excerpt *Seeking Fortune* by Josie Riviera

*R*ead the rest of Valentina's Story
Pick up your copy of Seeking Fortune today!
FREE on Kindle Unlimited!

*A*lso:
The Seeking Series

*S*avor the magic of the Romany Gypsies with this collection of romances in my exclusive 3 book bundle.

Find out why readers are falling in love with The Seeking Series & staying up all night reading! These Christian Regency romances will warm your heart.